Recreate
the elegant
world of
the Wild Rose
Inn with this beautiful stencil. . . .
Use it to decorate stationery,
furniture, your bedroom,
or any place you want
to add a touch of
timeless grace.

Warily, Ann raised her eyes to Roger's face. "Are you the king's man today?"

Roger smiled. "Not when I am with you."

She caught her breath. Their eyes held for a moment until Ann had to look away. A tremor went through her.

"A mate of yours is to be hanged," she said harshly.

"Ann—"

"He loved a Marblehead girl and would elope with her," she went on in a rush, hating herself for speaking, hating him for being British. "The fool. The fish-headed fool."

Roger winced. "He lost his heart."

"He'll lose his life now, too!"

Ann drew in a shaky breath. Had she lost her senses, she wondered, to have spoken so to a British sailor, to a man who might have shot her brother?

ANN OF THE WILD ROSE INN

JENNIFER ARMSTRONG

BANTAM BOOKS

New York • Toronto • London • Sydney • Auckland

RL5, age 10 and up

ANN OF THE WILD ROSE INN, 1774

A Bantam Book/February 1994

Wild Rose Inn™ is a trademark of Daniel Weiss Associates, Inc.

ISBN 0-553-29867-4

Published simultaneously in the United States and Canada

Bantam Books are published by Bantam Books, a division of Bantam Doubleday Dell Publishing Group, Inc. Its trademark, consisting of the words "Bantam Books" and the portrayal of a rooster, is Registered in U.S. Patent and Trademark Office and in other countries. Marca Registrada. Bantam Books, 1540 Broadway, New York, New York 10036.

PRINTED IN THE UNITED STATES OF AMERICA

OPM   0 9 8 7 6 5 4 3 2 1

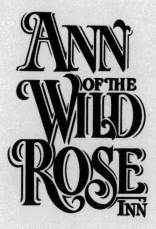

ANN
OF THE
WILD
ROSE
INN

Chapter One

ANN MACKENZIE THREW herself down onto the sand in the shade of a boulder. "I am glad to be quit of the Reverend Meacham for this day," she sighed. "I say 'tis hot enough without his sermons."

"Aye. If I hear one more sermon against the infamy of the British, I'll scream," Reliance Braxton agreed as she took off her shoes and stockings, her pale hair falling wispily into her face.

"Don't forget the British are our enemies," Judith Deane said. "Mr. Meacham is right to preach against them."

Reliance hunched her shoulders, tucking her chin into her chest in imitation of their turtlelike minister. "The Anglican Church has the effrontery to send missionaries to us," she mimicked, opening her eyes wide. "They dare send the Society for Propagat-

1

ing the Gospel in Foreign Parts to us? To us, whose fathers carried the Gospel into this wilderness among the heathen savages—"

"Enough!" Ann broke in with a scandalized laugh. She shielded her eyes against the brilliant light that danced off the Atlantic waters. "Reliance, you go too far."

"I thought he would burst his buttons," Judith admitted, sitting down next to Ann. "But I have heard the Anglicans wish to send bishops," she continued. "Can you imagine? Here in the Massachusetts Bay Colony? The Harvard divines must be ready to pop."

"Oh, fiddle," Reliance said, hitching up her skirts and splashing her feet in the water. "I don't care what church we attend, Church of England, Congregation of the Church of the Great Horny Devil." She picked up a scrap of seaweed and tossed it at Judith.

Judith screamed. "Pray God your pious father never hears you say that!"

"A hundred years ago you'd have been hanged as a witch for such heresy," Ann pointed out.

"I don't care a scrap," Reliance insisted. "So long as the Sabbath is kept as a day of rest, 'tis all one to me. Oh, to have a day with no work! How I had the bad luck to be apprenticed to such a stick as Mistress Upton I'll never know. She works me harder than any slave."

"You think your mistress is a raw burden. I'll tell you," Judith began.

As her two friends traded grievances about their apprenticeships, Ann lay back on her elbows and let their talk drift over her. She alone among them was not serving the strict terms of a legal apprenticeship, for she worked at home in her family's tavern. The Sabbath was no day of rest for her, but a busy workday, and she knew she must soon return to the Wild Rose Inn.

But for the moment, letting the hush of waves and the breeze and the keening of gulls and kittiwakes fill her ears, she could imagine herself a young girl again without a care. If she closed her eyes, she and her friends were children scrambling among the blueberry bushes or hiding among the sea-carved rocks and hunting for starfish, calling out childish challenges to one another.

"Perhaps I'll marry soon and can say farewell to Mistress Upton," Reliance said in a provocative tone.

Ann's visions fled in a rush, and Judith gave Reliance a startled look. "What do you mean by that, I wonder?" Judith asked. She lifted her hem as a wave foamed around her ankles.

"You haven't been asked, have you?" Ann said in surprise. "We—you're only sixteen."

Reliance only smiled again. "Is that too young to have a sweetheart, Judith?"

Judith blushed to the roots of her fiery hair and

Ann sat abruptly, tucking her knees up to her chin. "I doubt I will marry," she said with a frown. "There's not a boy in Marblehead I'd have."

"Perhaps you'll marry an Englishman," Reliance teased.

"Reliance!" Judith laughed.

Ann shook her head. "John believes—"

"Oh!" Reliance snapped her fingers in Ann's face. "John this, John that. You and your brother may be twins, but you needn't rely on him for every thought that you have."

"But I agree with him," Ann said.

"With every hotheaded patriotic notion he's got?" Reliance pressed, her blue eyes bright. "Come, he wants nothing more than to be a Son of Liberty. I believe he'd run off to Boston to dance a hornpipe under the Liberty Tree—if there weren't such a pretty reason for him to stay here in Marblehead." She sent a sly look at Judith.

Ann stubbornly shook her head again. "The British wrong us. Their warships ply the coast, confiscating our boats and pressing our own fishermen into the King's Navy against their will. And so much more have they done against us. John is right to hate them."

"Well I don't hate them," Reliance said. She sat to dry her wet feet with her stockings, and her forehead puckered with sudden gravity. "All this sedition and rebellion will disappear, and they'll be our friends once more."

"Perhaps," Ann said moodily. She traced a question mark in the sand and frowned at it. Then she wiped it away. "Perhaps."

Ann worked through the steaming noontime and dusty afternoon and hot evening, serving ale and China tea and wine at the Wild Rose Inn. But with the darkness she took herself off, slipping unnoticed through the streets of Marblehead and out along the Neck.

A breath of wind off the ocean touched her cheek as she stepped carefully from stone to stone along the beach. The only light was the faint glimmer of stars that rocked on the tidal pools. Low voices came to her as she stepped down onto wet, yielding sand.

"Curse you for a rogue and a knave and a British bootlicker, Nat Trelawney."

"I'll run you through, you rebel American dog," came a growl of laughter.

Ann's skirts trailed along broken shells with a faint scrape. The voices stopped.

One of them, sharp with threat, came out again. "Who is it?"

"Only me, John," Ann said.

Against the blackness of the sky and the shining, shifting darkness of the Atlantic, Ann's twin brother stepped lightly forward. "What do you here?" he asked. "This is no place—"

"Hsst," whispered his companion, Nat.

They paused, listening. Around them were the nighttime voices of the ocean: the lap and trickle of water through shell and stone, and the soft slap of waves reaching for the hull of a beached dinghy. There was nothing else, though Ann strained for any unfamiliar sound and almost fancied she heard the stealthy slide of ramrods down musket barrels. Smuggling quickened the imagination.

"I hear nothing," John said at last, but his voice was pitched softly.

"It may be they won't come," Ann suggested.

"They'll come," Nat murmured. "They'll signal."

Her brother squeezed her arm in a quick grasp. "Go home if you can't abide the waiting."

Ann shook her head, though her mouth tasted bitter with apprehension. "I'll bide here. We can look three ways now instead of only two."

"So cautious," John teased.

"As you refuse to be, so I'm cautious for both of us."

Ann could picture her brother's grin in the darkness as he took her hand and swung her arm to and fro. "I'm glad you're here, then," he said gently before letting go. "It has always been us two, hasn't it?"

"Aye, John," Ann whispered. "So it has."

The three were silent again, waiting, watching. The breeze stroked Ann's damp cheeks. She drew each breath with slow care and felt for her brother's hand in the dark. His fingers twined through hers, and together they awaited a ship carrying rum and molasses from the Indies, awaited a cargo to slip in past the thwarted English coast guard, awaited the chance to spit in the faces of their enemy. The transaction and trade would take place without benefit of papers, forms, and official ink. It was a hangable offense.

Ann's fingertips prickled as she looked out to sea. Each moment that her brother engaged in such perilous errands was an age to her, and she ached for it to be over. Now he withdrew his hand from around hers and paced along the beach.

"When will they come?" John demanded impatiently.

"Moon'll be up, soon," Nat said. "They must signal 'fore long, or we're out of it for this night."

"Yes," Ann said quickly. "It does not—"

"See!" John hissed.

Out to the northwest a light showed on the water, blinked, and was shuttered. Then, a moment later, it showed again and flickered into darkness. Ann's heart leaped and knocked against her ribs. She prayed it was no trick or trap.

"Is that it?" she asked. "Is it the proper signal?"

"Aye," John said, his voice exultant.

His footsteps and Nat's crunched over the shingle as they made to launch the dinghy and row out to receive their cargo. Ann, ever watchful, scanned the deep darkness for any sign of a British ship running without lights.

Then there was a scuffle and a soft splash, and John cried out in pain. Ann ran to the dinghy, stepping into the water.

"Of all the clumsy fools," John cursed himself.

"What is it?" Ann asked, feeling the suck of the waves dragging at her skirts. She clutched the gunwale of the rocking boat and sensed rather than saw her brother in the water beside her, gripping his arm.

Muttering furiously, John flexed his wrist. He gasped with pain. "I slipped and cracked my arm against the gun'l."

"Ah. You can't go out, now," Ann breathed.

"I can row," he said. " 'Tisn't even a sprain."

"Not against the tide, you can't," Nat said. "Nor if we're chased."

"Stop me, then," said John, swinging his leg over. He could never be stopped, ever, when he had decided to do a thing. "I've an appointment with the *Naumkeag*."

"We'll keep it for you." Ann gathered up her dripping skirts, and then hauled herself awkwardly over the side. The small boat dipped and rocked beneath her, crunching on the wet shingle of the beach. "I'll row."

"Annie, you can't," her brother said.

"Can't I, John MacKenzie?"

Nat shoved the boat further into the water. "Let her. Time flies."

While Ann hefted one of the pairs of oars, her brother climbed into the bow, still cursing his bad luck and his worse pain. With one last lurch, the boat made water and steadied itself, Nat jumping in at the stern.

"Put your back to it, Ann," Nat said, seating himself with the other oars.

Ann did not answer. She did not completely like Nat nor trust him. He was a spry, small, stealthy fellow, from a shifty family. Naturally John thought him a grand good fellow. Ann knew nothing against him save for his ready willingness to break British laws, but she did not feel easy in his company.

The tide was running strong and willful, and Ann pulled hard against it. The two pairs of oars rubbed dully in the muffled oarlocks, and the quiet dip and splash of their blades sounded like the regular jump of night-leaping fish running before the dolphin.

"Port," John murmured from the bow. "Gently aport."

Ann was rowing as hard as she could with her back to the ocean and could see only the lights of

Marblehead and not their destination. As the harbor slipped steadily astern, Ann yearned toward home, her eyes on the lights that blinked and winked as the masts of harbored ships swayed to and fro.

Then she ducked her head, pulling against the tide, and felt the water slide beneath them. She wished they might row on forever, out of touch of the smugglers' ship, past the coasting British, away from all those who were making her twin brother a stranger to her.

"Come on, Allender, you English pirate," John said with a wicked laugh. "Catch me if you can."

"Hush, John," Ann warned over her shoulder. "Don't court danger."

John only chuckled softly. Captain Allender commanded the *Southampton*, the navy schooner that hunted in Marblehead waters. He was the man John, Nat, and their like had sworn to bedevil at every chance. Ann feared him, feared his relentless pursuit, his arrogant scorn, and his steady hatred of the American cause.

"Up oars," John said hoarsely.

Ann and Nat stilled their rowing, and their craft bobbed in the swells, rocking as a cradle rocks. The oars dripped into the black waves, and Ann craned around to stare into the August night. At first she could see nothing. Then, resolving slowly into a form of black against black, the merchantman

Naumkeag loomed near, lightless and silent. The current of Ann's blood raced in her veins.

Nat cupped his hands to his mouth and whistled, and they waited again for several minutes. Then furtive sounds reached their ears from the smugglers' ship: the strain and creak of the yards, the wooden knocking of tackle and block, and the slow, deliberate snap of a flag moving in a gust of wind. A pulley squeaked, and another small craft hit the water with a soft splash. Ann heard oars dip and pull.

She steadied their own boat with her oars, scarcely breathing, and looked anxiously around for the British. She had a morbid certainty that Allender would appear at the moment John opened his arms for the contraband. Ann breathed deep and clenched the oars to keep her hands from shaking.

When the two vessels met, Ann kept her face turned away, her eyes aching with the strain of staring into the night. Quiet voices spoke in the dark, and Ann braced herself while the dinghy bucked and danced under the loading of heavy casks.

"Passengers," a voice said as the half-moon lifted itself above the horizon and rocked on its back like a white boat. "Squire Rum and Mistress Molasses. And a fragrant friend of theirs, too, a Chinaman."

"Here, hand over," John said.

"Your arm," Nat warned.

11

"It's nothing," John scoffed.

Ann kept her gaze fixed on the rising moon as the loading continued. Suddenly a dark, tall-masted shape slid across its white path and disappeared. Ann's heart gave a sickening leap.

"John, see! A ship!"

Her brother let out an oath, and there was a thump and sharp crack. Ann's feet were instantly awash. She dropped her oars and yanked up her skirts in panic when she realized it was rum.

"Take care!" Her hem was soaked, and the pungent smell clouded around her face. She coughed, dizzy from the fumes. Her heart was pounding.

"What ship?" came a fierce whisper.

Ann grappled with the oars again as the boat rocked on the swells, and tried desperately to see again the stealthy gliding shape. "Schooner-rigged, tacking this way I think," she said breathlessly.

"Was it the *Southampton*?"

Ann's mouth was dry with fear. "I could not see more than that."

The men were silent and still. The schooner might even now be bearing down on them. Ann counted her heartbeats as she scanned the black waters.

"You're certain of it?" Nat asked softly. "It wasn't a sounding whale you saw?"

Ann clenched the oars. "Certain. I've never seen a schooner-rigged whale, Nat."

"Right. We're away, then," said one of the *Naumkeag*'s men.

"What, so soon?" John replied lightly. "Won't you take a sip of this rum? Only dip your hand into our bilges."

"John, you fool," Ann muttered. She had to work to steady the boat, and could not keep her feet and dress out of the rum. She would reek of it, she knew, and must do something before she went home.

"Pray I don't get drunk from the smelling of it," she muttered, plying her port oar to turn the boat more into the inrushing tide.

"You won't go singing and carrying on in the town street, will you, Annie?" John teased.

"Singing songs of my wild willful brother, maybe," she retorted, her voice sharp with fear. "Now can we be away before Allender overruns us?"

She dug her long oars into the water, turning so sharply that their heavy-laden boat thumped hard against the *Naumkeag*'s dinghy as it pulled away.

"Steady, Ann," John said.

"Hold your voice down," she replied fiercely. "Must you call the navy at the tops of your very lungs?"

John laughed softly but did not speak.

Now, facing the open sea and the invisible schooner, Ann tried to blot out her fear and keep her nerves and her course steady. Her hands smarted, and an ache stretched across her shoulders and down each arm. The small craft was heavy with smuggled wares and hard to row, and would be easily overtaken in open waters. None of them spoke. Ann knew they all watched their wake, ready to jettison the cargo at the first sign of pursuit. The moon stretched itself out to them, lighting them for anyone to see. Ann hauled on the oars, although her back was on fire.

"See you anything?" Nat asked John.

"No, nor does anything see us," John muttered wryly. "He's a slow fellow, whoever he is."

Ann gritted her teeth. "*John*," she warned.

They spoke no more until they drove the boat aground in a sheltered cove north of the town. But Ann could still not quell the panic that was in her. She felt light-headed from the rum and the fear and her own exertion.

"Take a strong care," John said to Nat, springing out of the boat. He offered his hand to Ann, but she refused it, climbing out by herself.

"I'll stow it. You know where," Nat said.

Ann began climbing the steep shore, her sodden dress clinging to her legs. With mounting impatience, she hitched her wet skirts over her knees.

"What makes you so sharp tonight?" John asked, striding carelessly along beside her.

Ann's anger suddenly ran out of her and vanished, leaving only fear and an aching tiredness behind. When she turned to face her brother, the low moon touched his features with a slanting, faint light. His eyes glittered with it.

"John, don't go out again." She took his hand. "The danger is too great."

"Annie, little hen," John said tenderly. "There's no danger."

"No danger? Do you think me a fool?" she asked, dropping his hand in vexation. "What did we just break our backs for, running from that ship?"

"It may well have been American. We don't know it was Allender at all. I say it was no danger."

"You wouldn't be smuggling at all if there were no danger," Ann said wearily.

"Not so, for I'm determined to thwart those prying English. They must poke their noses into everything we do, telling us what trades we may practice and what we may manufacture, what laws we may make and how we judge ourselves. When they wish to punish us they suspend our assemblies and our legislatures. Do you not see I *must* go against them, Ann? And this way suits me."

"The greatest risk suits you."

"Ann, if you don't care for political reasons—"

"I *do* care for the political reasons," Ann broke in, "and I feel them full as strongly as you do."

"But they do not weigh with you in this, so listen to sense," John insisted. "Our family depends on rum and wine and tea. There would be no trade at the Wild Rose without them. So to save on the cost is a service to us MacKenzies."

Ann sighed at his obstinacy. She had heard all his arguments before. "But John, you're breaking the law—"

"British law, not ours," John broke in. "They've blockaded Boston Port, my sister, and moved the customs house to Salem. How can we let the chance go by, when the cargoes come in at our own back door?" He continued climbing the steep and rugged rocks.

Ann struggled to keep up with him. The chests of tea thrown into Boston Harbor at the Christmastide "Tea Party" still sent ripples across the water. Now oceangoing ships had to make harbor in Salem to pay duty, and Boston was bottled up. No ships but coasting vessels could make port in Boston, and those ships had to stop in Marblehead to be checked.

So local men with hardy boats and strong nerves went out to meet the great oceangoing traders before those ships made Salem. Out there in the coastal waters the cargoes of rum, tea, fine fabrics, and spices—all the stuff of the good life that had to pay heavy importation duties—these cargoes were lightened. Most 'Headers thought untariffed wares from the transatlantic trade ample reward for dodging the authorities.

The path soon brought Ann and John out on

top of a bluff outside town. Ann looked back, out at the Atlantic. Somewhere in the hot, still night, the smugglers' ship glided through the water. Somewhere also was the schooner that might well be a coast guard, tacking back and forth, around the rocky, small islands, along the convolutions of the coastline, searching, searching—for John. Ann drew in her breath sharply and smelled the reek of rum rising from her feet.

"Ann," John said, guessing her thoughts and softening to her. "Ann, I take all the caution I need. I'll never be caught, I promise."

"Promise me you'll leave off. The schooner—if it was Allender—" Ann's voice caught in her throat. "Promise me you'll not go out again."

"Ann, I cannot."

She pressed her hand to her hot brow. "I can't move you in this, then?" she asked sadly.

"You know I will not be moved," he replied. "I'm sorry that it gives you pain, but these are painful times."

"But Allender—"

"Let us say that it was Allender you spied," John said. "Pity the man, hunting for someone who isn't there. We go home, take our supper, greet our friends, and he is in the dark, chasing shadows."

Ann grinned in spite of herself. "I wish him joy of it."

17

"And who can say, it may begin to rain," John added with a rich laugh.

Then he took her arm and linked it through his, starting a fast walk down into Marblehead. Ann was not at all appeased, but she would not argue with her brother, for she hated to be out of accord with him. For all their lives, their thoughts and desires had been the same. Of late, however, with British meddling and managing on the rise, John had grown deaf to her wishes. She knew he would not stop until the British were routed.

"I wish the king and his blasted Parliament at the bottom of the ocean," Ann sighed as they neared town.

John laughed again. "Ah, you see we do agree."

Up ahead were lights and life and barking dogs, the activity of Marblehead. The Little Harbor, with its pebbled beach, was to their left. John held Ann back.

"You smell, darling sister, like a drunken bawd."

"And who gets the thanks for that?" she asked.

"It's me, it's me, I'm a shameful scapegrace," John sang, leading her to the water's edge. "But still and all, it wouldn't do to have you smelling of smuggled rum when we get home."

Ann stepped into the sharp-scented tidal water. "And does smuggled rum smell different?"

"Sweeter," her brother said, pulling her in with

both hands. "Sweeter, lassie, for it's untainted by the foul reek of the British."

Ann let him pull her, feeling the cool water rise up to her knees, feeling her dress billow and swell outward in the drink, and could not help but laugh as he cut a few dancing capers and made a mock bow. It felt good to be wet, to wade in the dark ocean under a rocking moon in the hot night. John was an old expert in chasing away her glooms, and she almost resented that he could cheer her so. Her anger washed away.

"I vow you'll smell of nothing but the good Atlantic, now," John said.

"And I vow you'll wash the brine from this dress, John," Ann laughed, slapping her hand through the water to splash him. Then she screamed as he lunged toward her, and she struggled back out of the water toward land, laughing and gasping, John sloshing by her side.

She gained the beach, and water streamed from her, gleaming silver in the moonlight. She smiled at the sky.

"Come," John said, following her out and catching his breath. "I've acquired such a thirst I'll drink brine in a moment. We may drink a toast to Allender, poor soul, hunting the perilous Nobody in the dark."

Grinning, Ann flicked the seawater off her fingertips into John's face, and he ducked and grabbed her hand. They ran together down Front Street, making for a broad, clapboard building with light and noise pouring from the open windows. With home in view, Ann hung back, not yet ready to step into the commotion that was the Wild Rose Inn.

"I'll go in the kitchen way," she said, reaching out for the gate in the fence.

"You will not," John said with bold heartiness. "We've had a fine night this night, and we'll walk through the front door and smile to all of our father's guests."

"John, no." Ann made for the gate again, but John grabbed her hand, and dragging her behind him, burst into the tavern. Ann stumbled in, blinking in the light. Before her were blue navy coats, and Captain Allender.

Chapter Two

THE RACE AND gallop of conversation hardly broke stride as brother and sister entered the Wild Rose Inn. Ann, her clothes still dripping, did not dare to look at the British officer, but she was too shocked to move.

"John MacKenzie, come in!" cried out a hearty voice. "Come, Annie darling!"

John put his hands on Ann's back. "So it wasn't him at all," he murmured, his smile wide for the assembly. "Go in." He nudged her, and she took a few hurried steps toward the kitchen door.

"Mistress Ann, hold there."

Captain Allender came forward and stood in her way. His eyes were on her—on her blond hair and flushed cheeks—and she knew he meant to woo her. He was young for his command, and arrogant with it, sure that gold braid and polished buttons were attractions enough for any colonial girl.

"Excuse me, sir," Ann said, her gaze fixed on his buckled shoes. Water was pooling around their feet from her wet dress, and her heart hammered in her ears. Surely he would smell the rum on her, standing uncomfortably close as he was. Her fears came cresting back on her again, and she could not help looking for her brother in the crowded room. He noticed her standing by Allender, and frowned.

"You've had a ducking, it seems," the captain began, his voice warm and insinuating.

"I have, and I must change my clothes," she said, pushing past him.

He grabbed her arm, and when she turned, his brown eyes were not so friendly. "Tell your father my men require more ale."

"Tell him yourself," John said rudely, taking Ann's defense and her other arm at the same time.

Ann yanked both her arms away, and slipped between them. Friendly voices called out to her and to John, but she hurried through the noisy room without answering them. She had always felt at home within the laughter and fellowship of the tavern, but the presence of the *Southampton*'s men now spoiled it for her. And of late, Allender's attention had made her work into a dreaded chore. Ann fled through the door into the hot kitchen, away from the noise.

"Why does Father serve him and his men?" Ann breathed, leaning her back against the door and closing her eyes. She had to compose herself, for her knees trembled and her skin was hot. She was still shaken by seeing Allender in her home and not harmlessly chasing shadows on the ocean as she had thought.

Her mother scarcely looked up from the kneading trough where she worked on the next day's bread. "The British have money," she said, her voice curt. "I can balance the accounts as well with their coin as with anyone else's."

"Oh, but I hate them, I hate that man," Ann whispered.

Mistress MacKenzie quirked one eyebrow. "You may hate them all you like or dance reels with them, but be here when I need you. We've a great deal of custom this night and you're wanted to serve. I cannot have you always slipping away as you do."

She stood up, wiping the back of one floury hand across her heated brow. Ann's mother was blond-haired, too, with the clear blue eyes and strong, handsome features that the twins had inherited. Still, Ann felt no closeness to her.

Eyeing Ann's dripping clothes, Mistress MacKenzie added, "And if you go aboating this time of night, you might fall into the drink and never be found, my girl."

Ann regarded her mother steadily. Mistress

23

MacKenzie knew full well what errands John and Nat carried out at night, and did nothing to stop them. "It'd be a blessing to me," Ann said in a stony voice.

With that, she left the room by another door and climbed the dark staircase to the second floor.

Upstairs, she closed herself in the sanctuary of her own room, a tiny chamber at the front of the house with a window overlooking the harbor. Yet even there the hum and babble of voices reached through the floorboards to her. She closed her ears to it and flung the window open wide for the breeze and the moon's kind light.

They were rare, the moments when Ann had time to herself, and so she craved solitude. The only company she could abide for very long was her brother's, and Judith and Reliance's, and that of her mild-spoken father. To be the daughter of an inn-keeper seemed a bitter fate to her. She must always be on call, ready to serve and carry, with never a moment for her own thoughts.

Quickly Ann stripped and changed into the second of her three summer dresses, and leaned her elbows on the windowsill.

Out beyond the harbor was the Neck, a crooked arm that stretched around from the main-land to shelter the port, and beyond the rocky Neck was the wild wide ocean under the black sky. Ann loved to imagine the ships that were out there on the main at night and took comfort in their tiny courage in the darkness. Just specks they were, at the mercy of the great sea, and yet they plied onward. Sometimes Ann thought of herself that way, sailing through Marblehead, steering her course in a sea of people and politics, looking for safe harbor in a place gone suddenly unfamiliar.

She did not know how, in such a short time, everything had changed. The British, once their brothers, had become heavy-handed landlords, scouting the coast. The people of Massachusetts had grown suspicious and quick to anger. The folk of Marblehead had become cruel and watchful when English ships foundered off her rocky shores in bad weather, waiting for good scavenging instead of manning the lifeboats. And John, her brother John, her strongest ally in childhood adventures—now he often had a look in his eyes that Ann did not recognize.

And so when she looked at the ocean of late, there was worry in her heart. She feared that the home of her early years was slipping away from her, that she had somehow let the lines drop from her hands and could never regain them. With a sigh, she pushed herself away from the window and left the room.

Still in darkness, Ann made her way along the passage. It changed in level where new rooms had been added onto the Wild Rose. What had begun as a simple, four-room building had grown as the town had grown, and some locals joked that new additions appeared on the house, clinging like limpets, with every low tide. The Wild Rose now boasted extra chambers for traveling guests, a third floor, and an attic. Ann's grandfather had overseen the digging of a large, cool cellar for storing barrels of ale, and there was now another staircase leading down into the new parlor. That room was reserved for distinguished company and seldom used, and for that reason it was always quiet. Down the corridor, then around a corner, and Ann stepped into the inky stairwell.

She gathered her skirts in one hand and trailed the other along the oak-paneled wall as she descended in the stuffy dark. With her thumb on the iron latch at the bottom, she paused, listening, and then swung the door open and looked into the empty parlor.

The room was filled with pale moonlight, as cool as the ashes in the dead hearth, and the tavern sounds were muted like voices of ghosts. The very beams and shingles of the house seemed alive around her. Ann could almost imagine her grandfather sitting there by the fire, speaking of the inn's early days and of his lost sister, Bridget.

"Always laughing she was when she arrived from Scotland in 1695," he used to say. "And her wild tumbling hair all about her face. She was like a fairy queen of delights to me then, and I such a little boy. I loved her at once and still do."

But Bridie MacKenzie had loved where she should not have loved and was accused of witchcraft by the mother of Will of God Handy. So Bridie had taken herself away to Canada, where she finally did marry and thrive. But Ann's grandfather, John, could never forgive the Handys for driving his singing sister from Marblehead. He had died six years past, calling Bridie's name.

And now Ann could almost hear that sigh in the cool, still room. Then there was a footfall, and she shrank back.

A figure loomed in the doorway opposite to her, silhouetted by the faint light of the passage. "Ann?"

Ann shook her head impatiently. "What do you lurk about here for, Tom Handy?"

"I carry a word from your father," said the great-grandson of Will of God. "He asks you to hurry back."

"And I don't doubt you're the one pestering him to know where I was," Ann said.

"Annie, Annie." Tom advanced slowly. "Such a touch-me-not you are. We should be gentle to one another, Ann. Our families go back together a long time."

"I will thank you to touch me not," Ann retorted. She walked past him to the door. "You've a business of your own to attend at the ship. Go back there and leave off trying to coax my father's guests to your own sorry establishment. There has never been any 'together' between us and you."

Ann shut the door on him and headed for the noisy front room, catching her apron from its hook on the wall as she went. She knew the night's stresses were telling on her, for her voice was sharp and her hands shook. If her brother did not stop his adventuring soon, she feared she would go mad. Drawing an unsteady breath as she tied her apron, she braced herself as though for battle. Then she pushed open the door onto the roar of the tavern.

"The king may be a good man for all I know," one man near her was saying. "And who's to question the sovereign?"

"But there are those that have his private ear," countered another, punctuating his words with a finger in the first man's chest. "And they whisper and contrive to have him grant royal favors and monopolies to our disadvantage."

"Ah, Annie my dear," Mr. MacKenzie said, seeing her by the door. "Carry this to Mr. Talbot."

Ann took the pewter mug of ale from her father's hands and crossed the room for Josiah Talbot's table. All around her, voices rose with the smoke, their accents mixed and varied. There were Cornish voices and Irish, Shetlander and Welsh, Scottish and Devonshire and Wessex and all, blending together in the great American Tower of Babel. The men gathered in the Wild Rose were fishermen and merchants, smiths and ropemakers, coopers and boatwrights, and each and every man had his opinion of the latest colonial grievances.

"I say treat us as English subjects with all the rights thereto!" a peg-legged, pipe-smoking seaman declared loudly. "Or they may relinquish claim to our loyalty. One way or another we will not let them tax us at the whim of every villainous dandy in the House of Lords."

Ann avoided looking over at Allender and his men, but she knew they attended to every hot word and stored up the slanders for later use. As long as no one openly called for treason and sedition, nothing could happen. She squeezed herself by two wildly gesturing opinionators and set the mug down in front of her father's old friend.

"Thank you, Ann, and how are you this night?" Josiah Talbot asked.

"Well, sir. Good evening, Mr. Penworthy," she added to his companion.

Penworthy had both elbows on the table, and his fine linen shirt was damp with sweat. His horsehair wig, long in need of redressing, was pushed carelessly to the back of his head. "It'd be a better evening if Allender departed," he said, vigorously scratching his freckled scalp.

"I do agree with you," Ann said. "Most strongly."

She stood still for a moment as the sea of voices continued to swell and swirl around her, and she scanned the crowd by habit for her brother. Penworthy and Talbot picked up their conversation where they'd left off.

"There's some in Boston who think the tea should be paid for," Talbot said, gazing down into his ale. "With the port closed, the town is full of jobless men, families turned out of their homes and all things scarce."

Penworthy snorted. "All things scarce but British meddling," he said. "The Crown is poking its nose into a hornets' nest."

"I'd say Talbot has already done that," joked a man sitting nearby.

Laughter met this comment, and Talbot himself joined in. His nose was as red as a boiled lobster.

"It wasn't hornets made Talbot's nose glow," chimed in another. " 'Twas the price of rum."

"Then the color is sure to wax pale as the price goes higher," a sailor named Gant put in.

"That's true," Talbot said. "Imported rum costs a criminal price, no offense to my host, MacKenzie!"

Tom Handy had placed himself among the jokers, and he caught Ann's eye. "The price of rum—the price of importation is very steep, isn't it, Ann?"

Ann heard the sly hint in his voice and stepped

back so abruptly into Reliance's father that she knocked a mug of ale from his hand. It spilled on her own dress, and she bit back a cry of dismay.

"Not again!" she wailed, shaking the liquor from her skirt in vain. "I beg pardon, Mr. Braxton."

She started away, but Tom spoke up. "How *again*, Ann?"

Several men stopped speaking, and there was a swift exchange of glances before Talbot brought his mug down on the table with a bang. "Poor lass is likely to be drowned in ale with this rabble tossing their drink around. I say toss it down your own throat, or if you must throw it somewhere else, I've a mouth always open!"

There was more laughter and slapping of backs, and Ann gratefully turned away from Tom Handy without answering.

With another hurried apology to Mr. Braxton, Ann began edging through the crowd again. But Captain Allender beckoned from the table where he sat alone, imperious and cold. A group of his midshipmen caroused at a table near him, but he held himself aloof. With a sinking heart, Ann made her way over.

"That red-faced oaf of a man has a big mouth indeed," Allender said with a sneer for Talbot. "He should be careful to keep it shut lest it land him in trouble."

"Mr. Talbot is a harmless man," Ann replied.

"And needs a beautiful girl to defend him, I see."

Ann ignored his flattery. She was afraid she might scream or burst into tears or throw a jug at the wall. She only wanted to get away.

"How did such an uncouth place produce a girl such as you?" Allender went on in a thoughtful tone. He put one foot up on a chair and steepled his hands. "You're made of finer stuff than this mean crowd, you know."

Her face burned, but she said nothing.

"Come, Ann," he continued, lowering his voice. "I have watched you now for two months. Is it not time we come to an understanding, you and I?"

"I don't know what you mean, sir."

"I think you do."

"I swear I do not!" Ann looked around her wildly, praying that none could hear. "I don't know your meaning, but I do know you wrong me."

Allender swung his feet down abruptly and leaned across the table on one elbow, his forehead creased. "You Americans are savages, the lot of you, no better than the red men. But we'll tame you, that I swear," he said through clenched teeth.

Stunned, Ann stepped backward from his cruel look.

"Now, now," came a pacific voice. Mr. MacKenzie hurried over. "What's amiss, Captain Allender?"

"Your daughter does not wish to serve me," Allender said, meeting Ann's eyes with cruel irony. "I only desire hot buttered rum."

"Annie, Annie," Master MacKenzie said. "The captain is our guest. You mustn't be backward—"

"That's not what he means," Ann broke in, her blood pounding in her ears.

"What's all this?" John joined them with a hard look of suspicion at the officer. "What does he say to you, Ann?"

"What I say to her is none of your business," Allender sneered, looking down his long nose at John.

"Leave my sister alone," John said hotly. "Or you'll know what business of mine it is."

The young captain only laughed, and Mr. MacKenzie held his hands out. "Now, now," he said. "John, see to Mr. Braxton. I fear he lost his drink."

For a moment John stood glaring at Allender, angry for Ann's sake. Allender turned his back and sat down again. "The rum, host, served plain. The relish of rhetoric and threat I can do without."

Ann turned and fled through the crowded room to the kitchen. Her father came in after her.

"Ann, why do you—"

"Father, his words have two meanings," Ann said, grabbing her father's arm. "Don't make me carry anything to him, please."

Her father's mild, gentle face puckered with

alarm. "But, Annie, what can you mean? I'm sure he's a gentleman."

"Gentleman?" Ann gaped at him. "Why are you so ready to bow and scrape to the British, Father? They only hurt us."

"Ah, but it may be we can come to an understanding," Mr. MacKenzie said.

Ann flinched at his unconscious echo of Captain Allender. Her soft-spoken father wanted peace and would pay any price for it, and that hurt her. Ann's mother stood at the fire, stirring a pot without comment.

"Sit you down, lass," her father said, pushing Ann into a chair. "Don't distress yourself. I'll see what he wants."

"I fear I know what he wants," Ann said forlornly. "He would—"

The door burst open, and John came in. "What was his insult?"

Ann felt his anger sweep through the kitchen. She glanced at her mother, who looked back with her eyebrows raised.

"He flirts and makes advances to me," Ann muttered. "He told Father I wouldn't bring him hot rum."

"I'll bring him a hot rum," John said. "But I'll poker it after he's drunk it down."

"That's enough." Mistress MacKenzie's voice cut

across the kitchen. "Don't make trouble in your father's house."

"But Father should throw them out," John insisted, banging his fist on the table. "As should all the Colonies. What use or need have we of pampered princelings and their armies? They only want to suck us dry."

Mistress MacKenzie laughed bitterly. "As long as they pay for what they drink."

"Mother, you're as bad as our father is," John complained.

"And how bad is that?"

While John and their mother argued, Ann sat staring into the hearth. She was for independence as much as her brother was, for anyone could see the Crown only took from them and never gave. They must be subject to unjust laws and restrictions, and could only indirectly plead their causes in Parliament. For these honors and privileges the colonists paid heavy taxes.

Ann knew the Patriots' cause was just. But as her brother abused England with all the oaths he knew, she thought of Bridie again, and the Scottish home that the MacKenzies left a hundred years earlier.

"Wouldn't you wish to see it, though?" she mused in a faraway voice, staring deep into the coals. "The springing heather and the eagles?"

John broke off and stared at her. "What, England?"

"Scotland," Ann said. Her dream dissolved as he stared disgustedly at her, and she looked away, hurt.

"No," John said. He took her hand in his and squeezed it so hard she winced. "This is our country, Ann, and I'll never want another."

She was swayed by the intensity of his feeling and by the strange bond that tied them together. She gripped his hand in return.

"Nor will I, John. As long as you're here."

Chapter Three

THE NEXT MORNING'S sun pressed onto the top of Ann's head. She stood in the back of the garden at a fire, stirring a cauldron of tallow and ashes into soap, and felt the heat drip down her back and her arms. Nearby the bees hummed dizzily in the lavender. The inn beside her seemed almost a live thing, dozing in the sun, letting off comfortable settling sounds in the heat, and breathing a burnt mineral smell from the gray paint. Windows stood open like flung nets waiting to catch any breeze that drifted past. Timbers for another addition to the inn lay nearby, smelling of sap. All was quiet, resting. Danger was at bay.

Ann raised her face to the hot white sky, sighed peacefully, and gave the pot another stir.

"I swear you'll melt into the pot yourself and

we'll use you to wash our clothes with," a voice behind her said.

Ann laughed and looked over her shoulder at Judith. "Keep a careful watch for me, then. And if I vanish, treasure this soap for special washings and think of me."

Judith pushed open the garden gate, breaking off a bloom from the gnarled rosebush that twined about the fence at the side of the inn. She sauntered in, twirling the stem between her fingers and putting her nose into the red petals. Wisps of her coppery hair had escaped its pins with the heat and floated lightly around her face.

"My love is like the red—soap?" Judith sang in a questioning tone, looking down into the kettle of gray, greasy muck.

"Of all the tasks my mother could set me today, it had to be soap," Ann said. "What a misery."

"I'd rather be digging clams, myself." Judith pinched the fabric of her bodice, holding it away from her skin.

"Why are you not working?" Ann asked, wiping her damp forehead with the hem of her apron.

Judith, who was apprenticed to a mantua-maker in the town, gave Ann an arch smile. "Who's to say I'm not working?" she said.

"You're not shirking, are you?" Ann asked, shocked. The rules for apprenticeships were strict and strong, and wayward apprentices could find themselves in the stocks.

Judith shook her head, bringing up the bright red rose again to smell. "I go to Mistress Devane. She has a pattern doll from England, and my mistress wishes to copy it. 'Tis hard to get the latest styles now that the shipping is so straitened. And so, to Mistress Devane I go."

"And if your way lies by our house, you must stop and see if I wish to place an order for three dresses, two mantuas, a chemise, and a pair of ribboned sleeves."

"And do you wish such items, m'lady?" Judith asked.

Ann laughed and gave the bubbling soap another hard stir. "Not today."

"Leave off that," Judith said. " 'Tis too hot to stand here by the fire."

"But it will lump." Ann wiped her face again. "Don't stay if you don't wish to."

Judith strolled a few steps off, idly swatting the tall tansy plants with her rose. Ann watched her friend from the corner of her eye and stirred—and waited.

"Where's John this morning?" Judith finally asked, not looking at Ann.

"He's here," John himself answered, leaning out a ground floor window with a cocky grin.

Judith flushed scarlet and dropped her rose in embarrassment. "What manner of spy are you?"

"The best kind. A good one."

"And what makes a good spy?" Judith retorted.

"Hearing what he wants to hear," John said, perching on the windowsill and gazing merrily down at her. He was eating an early apple and tossed another apple in his other hand for a moment. Then he tossed it down to Judith. She caught it deftly, her eyes sparkling with sudden excitement as she looked up at him.

"You didn't go to Cobb's orchard without me, did you?" Ann asked in astonishment. "We always go together."

John glanced at Ann sheepishly and then shrugged.

A bee, drunk with nectar, flew by Ann's cheek, hovered over the lush blown rose that lay on the grass, then crawled in among the scented petals. Ann blushed.

Judith turned her back on John and returned to the fire. "Haven't you noticed," she said loudly to Ann, "how handsome some of the British sailors are?"

Shocked, Ann glanced up to see how her brother would answer. His smile vanished, and he swung his legs out the window and jumped to the ground.

"What sedition is this?" he demanded, crossing the garden in three long strides.

Judith turned around with pretended surprise. "Oh, did you address me?"

"I did."

"But I did not address you," Judith said. "I was speaking to Ann."

"I've never found a one of them worth looking at twice," Ann said to pacify her quick-tempered brother.

"Nor will she ever," John said. He put one arm confidently across Ann's shoulders.

She shrugged him off. "I'm hot enough, thank you," she said. "And you know Judith only means to provoke you."

Judith smiled at Ann, ignoring John completely. "I saw a midshipman with a bold eye just this morning. And such a handsome uniform. Do you not believe blue the finest color on a man?"

"Judith," Ann said with a shake of her head. She tried not to smile but felt a laugh rising up in her.

John walked away to the end of the garden, and began hefting empty casks out of a shed. Ann and Judith watched him for a moment. Judith picked up her rose and raised it to her face. Ann could see her smile and dancing eyes and the edges of her white teeth as she caught her lower lip with them.

"You did say that only to provoke him, didn't

you?" Ann asked, giving the pot another stir. The soap was beginning to lump, in spite of her effort.

"Maybe so," Judith said. "But there is many a handsome British man, and you can't deny it."

"I can," Ann said seriously. "That race of men is branded and ugly to me."

"Oh, Annie." Judith looked seriously at her. "Do you mean to tell me that you'd let a man's country stop you from looking at him? What if he was the one man you could fall in love with? You'd never even know it."

Ann shook her head. "I know I couldn't love a British man. And anyway, I don't know what that means, to fall in love."

"You'll know when it happens," Judith said softly. Her gaze went back to John where he strained at the barrels, and she chuckled.

With a wry smile, Ann walked over to her brother. "You look as ridiculous as six drunken sailors," she said under her breath. "Showing off this way, it's absurd."

He laughed, and spat on his hands to tackle another cask. "But these barrels must be shifted."

"At precisely this moment when Judith is watching with such approval?" Ann said, shaking her head. "What a coincidence it is, Brother."

John arched his brows in mock surprise, but his blue eyes were brilliant with laughter. "Oh, is Judith watching?"

"Not any longer," their friend called. "I must be on my errand. Good-bye."

Ann watched Judith depart, the sun shining so brightly on her friend's red hair that it seemed to blaze. She was about to tease John further, but the expression on his face as he watched Judith made Ann forget her words.

A flush washed over her skin. "You might have *told* me you were going for apples," she said in a strangled voice. She dragged off her apron and flung it over a cask.

"I didn't think— Where are you off to?" John asked in surprise.

"To get some air," Ann muttered. She passed the kettle on its iron tripod over the fire and sent it a frown. "And you can lump all you like."

"Ann! I'm sorry! Wait!"

She ran from her brother's voice, out into Front Street where the women swept their narrow front steps and dogs quarreled over fish heads. Above, gulls perched on the ridgelines of the houses and lifted first one foot and then the other from the hot roofs.

As Ann walked along, she saw on every side the evidence of Marblehead's fishy trade: nets and boats, barrels for storing salted cod, gateposts fashioned from whale ribs. The business of the town was fish —fish and the merchant marine. In even the humblest house, rare exotics adorned the shelves. On

43

one doorstep in the sun lay the upper carapace of a giant sea turtle, filled with rising bread dough; on the windowsill of another house sat a heathen idol carved in some South Sea Isle from a spiced wood; and in yet another yard, a rich Turkish carpet hung airing from a line, side by side with a canvas sailor's shirt.

Ann saw these things, and yet she did not see them, for her mind was filled with a confusion of images. For the most part, she saw her brother's face and heard her brother's taunting voice. She knew she should be glad that Judith and John were steering courses that would soon meet; but still she felt hurt, out of sorts and out of place. She was jealous.

Walking slowly, her brows drawn together, Ann wondered if John took his risks for more than political reasons. She knew full well he was a Patriot to the core, yet his chosen battleground was in the smuggling coves, and his trophies benefited the tavern that would one day be his—and Judith's?

The thought that one day Ann's home might be Judith's domain startled her and deepened her frown. To remain at the Wild Rose for the rest of her days as servant to a friend was not a prospect anyone could welcome. Yet to avoid a gray spinsterhood meant leaving her home, perhaps even leaving Marblehead itself. And that she could not imagine.

In a strange, dark humor, Ann strayed down to the port. There, all was action and shouting, wares loading and unloading, sailors swarming around and above and within the ships and the rigging. Officials, their buttons winking in the sunlight and their faces glistening with sweat, waved and pointed and shouted commands. In spite of the tension that soaked into each meeting of American colonist and British officials, the business of the port continued unchecked. Ships were provisioned, wares were hauled, and the nimble, barefooted mariners sprang from ship to dock and spar to bowsprit as lightly as birds. The sky and the water reflected the bright sun up and down and everywhere, tossing light into every corner and hole. The creak of hawser and slap of wave was like the living pulse of the harbor itself. Squinting, Ann leaned against a pyramid of casks and let the ocean's great expanse take the heat away from her. Among this crowd she could be alone, for none took any notice of her.

Except one. "Annie! Thank God!"

She turned and saw Reliance beckoning from the shadow of a building. Ann walked over with a grateful smile. Wild Reliance would have some outrageous story to tell and would chase off that last of Ann's bad humor.

"If your father is lame today, it's because I trod on his foot last night," Ann said.

Reliance looked about her, her light blue eyes red-rimmed and nervous. "Oh, did you?" she murmured absently.

Ann frowned, studying Reliance's pale face. "Is something amiss?"

"No—only—" Reliance plucked at her apron with restless fingers. "I must ask you—have you any money, Ann?"

"Money? Not a shilling. You know my mother keeps all our accounts," Ann replied. She caught the habit of Reliance's nervous scannings like a yawn and darted a worried look over her own shoulder. "What is it?"

The young woman before her, ever a plain and sand-haired slip of a girl, was suddenly transformed into a beauty. She caught Ann's hand in a tight grip. "Tomorrow night I run away with my lover," she breathed.

"Reliance!" Ann shook her head. "What is this? What lover? Know your parents what you do?"

"No!" Reliance flattened herself against the shed wall and covered her eyes with one hand. "They don't know—they know nothing, and they would stop me."

"For you are still 'prenticed," Ann said.

"The devil can take that bitch of a seamstress," Reliance hissed. "That's not my fear."

Ann glanced furtively at a drunken sailor who had slumped against a coil of rope nearby. She stepped closer to her friend and looked searchingly into her eyes. "What, then? Who is this man, and why have you never told me?"

Reliance smiled, but her smile held some terror as well as joy. "He's British—a sailor of the *Southampton*," she whispered, her eyes wide.

"No . . ." Ann stared at Reliance, horrified. "You can't love one of Allender's men. They are the enemy. You *cannot* love one of them. It is wrong."

"But I do," the girl said, gripping Ann's hand tighter still. "I do, my very soul does love his and I must go with him. I did not seek this love. But I cannot hide from it."

"Reliance, this is not love, say it is not," Ann pleaded. "You are one of us."

Reliance shook her head. "I can't tell the difference between him and me anymore. There is none. If you cannot help me, please guard my secret."

Ann felt her back prickle with sweat. She licked lips gone suddenly dry and gazed everywhere but at Reliance. Here was a girl whom Ann had known since infancy. They had played and worked together and walked hand-in-hand. And though Reliance had always been impetuous and heedless, never had Ann suspected such solemn force and purpose within her friend. Reliance looked ready for battle, fiercely strong and brave and unflinching.

"Is this because you love him?" Ann whispered.

"Yes. Because I love him," Reliance repeated simply.

Ann's breath stuck in her throat. "I won't tell," she vowed.

"We must go far from here," her friend said.

"Am I never to see you again?" Ann felt her stomach turn sickeningly. "Reliance—you are too dear to me! How can I lose you?"

Reliance put her hand to Ann's cheek. "Do not forget me," she said. "Farewell."

"Farewell," Ann said. "God protect you."

The girls embraced, and in an instant, Reliance fled around the corner of the shed and vanished. Ann put one hand to her forehead and stepped back into the sunlight, wondering if she had dreamed the whole thing.

"Here's a friendly face," called a familiar voice.

She turned. An old friend of her parents', Captain Carter, was striding toward her through the crowd.

"Welcome home. When did you make Marblehead?" she asked.

"This morning, and what a welcome home I've had," he replied, casting a wary glance at the Crown's official presence.

"Please let us not talk about it," Ann said, brushing politics distressfully aside.

"That's well," the captain replied. He was a handsome man, with hair still thick and black and a face tanned like leather from years at sea. He dug in the gaping pocket of his long frocked coat, and pulled out what looked to be a cup of horn or shell. "And what do you think this is?"

Ann took it and turned it over in her hands. It was perfectly round, and hard and thin, open at the top. Light poured in through the translucent sphere and lay pooled within like gold. "I don't know."

"That, my girl, is the eyeball of a whale. And it came all the way from Nantucket."

Ann laughed. "A long voyage indeed."

"I bought it off a Negro harpooner," he said. "I thought it might please your mother."

Ann's smile faded and she looked uncomfortably away. Here was a man still full of charm and grace and derring-do, who must have set all girls' hearts knocking in his youth. Yet he had never married, and when he was in port he visited Ann's mother as though Mistress MacKenzie were still an unwed maid. Ann thought of her gentle father and clenched her fingers around the fragile cup.

"Sir," she began, her cheeks coloring. "Is there not some other woman you might bring this gift to?"

Captain Carter rubbed his chin and gave her a wry grin. "I believe I have just been put in my place."

"I mean no offense," Ann said. "But—"

"But it is not seemly for a reckless adventurer such as I to bring dainties to Matthew MacKenzie's wife," the captain continued, his eyes twinkling with good humor. "Don't fear, Ann. Your mother married a rare good man, and she knows it."

Ann smiled uncertainly at Captain Carter, resenting his attention to her mother but swayed by his charm.

"I never saw such a smile for me, maid," a voice intruded, "and I'd give up the king's shilling for it."

Captain Allender sauntered over, the sun gleaming on the brass buttons of his coat. His lips curled, and he looked from Ann to Captain Carter and back again.

"How friendly this parley seems," he said.

"Captain Carter is the friend of my childhood," Ann explained, holding the whale-cup behind her. However she felt toward Carter, at least they were united against the British officer.

Allender quirked one eyebrow. "What wares have you?"

"It is only a trinket from Nantucket," Captain Carter replied, "and needs none of your poking and prying."

"Allow me to be the judge of that," Allender said.

"It is truly nothing!" Ann shook her head. "I pray you, Captain Allender. Do not accost this man."

The gleam darkened in Allender's eyes as he lowered his lids halfway. "You seem always to be defending the men of this town. It is very strange to me that they must rely on a maid."

Ann glanced swiftly at Captain Carter and saw his jaw tighten in anger, but he only smiled.

"You see us as we are, harmless, tied to the

apron strings of the females. You'd do as well to sail away and not trouble over us anymore." Carter swept off his hat and bowed low in plain mockery.

Ann caught her breath, and all seemed to go quiet around them as she waited for Allender's response. But then the gulls yawked, and the shouts of seamen rolled out in waves, and all was breeze and light air again. Allender slowly withdrew his gaze from Carter and looked at Ann.

"As I give way before your defense of this man, you may remember to smile at me more softly when next we meet." The officer grinned without warmth and walked away.

Ann's fingers tightened around the cup, and she felt the heat spread along her back and neck. How could any woman love an Englishman, if this was an example? Captain Carter watched Allender depart, and when he spoke his voice was hard. "Does that man make advances to you?"

"It is truly nothing," she said again, anxious to smooth the waters again.

"It did not seem nothing, Ann."

She put her hand on his arm. "Sir, please. Forget that. And you must not put yourself into trouble by carrying gifts to any MacKenzie," she said, holding the cup out to him.

"No trouble," he said, his eyes lingering still on Allender's retreating figure. "I'll consider it an honor.

Please take it as a gift to all the MacKenzie clan, if you won't take it to your mother."

The day's heat pressed down on Ann. Reluctantly she lowered the cup to her side. "Very well," she said. "And now I must go home."

Ann turned her back on the harbor's clash and hurried along the streets to the Wild Rose Inn.

When she stepped into the dark kitchen, Ann paused to adjust her eyes. The glow of the hearth threw out a heat to rival the sun's. Mistress MacKenzie came into the room from the opposite door.

"A fine mess of soap you've made," Ann's mother said.

Ann rubbed her thumb along the smooth hardness of the whale-eye cup. She could not picture her mother ever soft enough for any man to woo. "Captain Carter bade me carry this to you."

She held out the cup, and Mistress MacKenzie reached her hand out slowly. "He's a fool," she said in a quiet voice.

"I believe so, too," Ann replied, jealous for her father's sake.

Her mother glanced at her sharply. "I never ask him to do it."

"Nor do you ever ask him not to."

"What he does is no business of mine," Mistress MacKenzie replied.

Ann sat down, propping her chin on one hand.

It was so hot she could scarcely breathe, let alone think clearly. She could not fathom that the man would persist in his devotion to a woman long married and harried by cares, and was of two minds whether she scorned or admired the captain for it.

Mistress MacKenzie held the cup to the fire's light and revolved it slowly in her hands. Her eyes softened, and a smile came to her mouth. Ann looked at her and felt hurt.

"Here's the truant," John called, coming into the kitchen with a hammer in his hand. He poured himself some beer from a pitcher and drank it lustily down. "Gallivanting about the town while Father and I work, Ann? You surprise me. What have you brought our mother?"

Mistress MacKenzie came to herself and with a frown set the cup on the mantelshelf among the pewter candlesticks and her dowry spoons. "Only a foolish geegaw from Captain Carter."

John set his tankard down, and his gaze went to Ann. "Our Captain Carter in port, is he?"

"Yes, and what of it?" Ann said tiredly. She scratched with one fingernail at the block of salt that stood in a saucer on the table.

"It may be he's brought me a token of his travels, too," John answered, giving her a wink.

Ann looked at him in instant understanding and felt the hairs on her arms prickle. She was suddenly sure that Captain Carter was in on the smuggling with John and Nat, and his arrival meant the battle against Allender was about to heat up.

John let out a lighthearted laugh and left the room, leaving Ann suddenly cold.

Chapter Four

ANN AROSE EARLY the next day. She stood at her window, watching the first stirrings of the town. Out in the harbor, a breeze rippled the water, and the air was still cool and fresh on her forehead. She rested her cheek against the frame of the window, absently running one finger back and forth along the sill. This had been Bridie's room, she knew. Standing at the window, looking out as Bridie must have done, always gave Ann a sense of kinship with her ancestor. Her grandfather had told such stories of Bridie that Ann had almost felt she knew her. It had once been her wish that Bridie, singing, smiling, Scottish Bridie, could have been her mother.

Now she simply wished for her as a friend. With a sigh, Ann left her room to begin her chores.

"I'll milk," she said, passing her mother in the kitchen and catching up an oak bucket.

She let herself out the back door and walked through the dew-damp garden to the cowshed. Inside the sweet dimness, Lace the cow slewed her head around to look at Ann, stretched her neck, and lowed.

"Coom, coom," Ann murmured, pulling a stool up to the cow's side. She rested her cheek against the animal's flank, feeling Lace's great heartbeat, and rhythmically pulled the milk into the bucket. It hissed as gently as a whisper.

"Good morning, Ann," came Mr. MacKenzie's voice.

Ann turned her head against the cow's side and smiled a greeting to her father.

"I wonder if I'll get a sup of that milk," he said.

"There's still some of yesterday's cooled in the cellar," Ann told him.

He found a wooden cup on a shelf and shook the dust from it. "Oh, I like it fine this way. I wouldn't think to improve on the gifts Lace brings us."

He dipped the cup into the bucket and sipped the milk contentedly. Ann laughed.

"If any of our patrons saw you now, they'd wonder how you brew such fine ale," she teased.

Mr. MacKenzie chuckled. "I know it. Milk may be fit for none but infants, but I've always had a taste for it. Now you keep it our secret, Annie, or next thing you know, folk will be saying I drink water, too."

"Father?"

"Yes, Annie?" Mr. MacKenzie stood in the doorway, framed by the morning light, the sun making an aura around his head.

"Was our mother once less hard than she is?" Ann asked in a low voice.

"Ah?" Her father leaned against the frame of the door, gazing down into his cup. "She always had a ready sharp tongue, mind you, and was ever of a managing manner."

Ann grimaced to herself.

"But never a comelier or livelier girl in Marblehead than Valor Bull," Mr. MacKenzie continued.

"Is that all a man looks for when he marries?"

Mr. MacKenzie turned his head aside for a moment, considering, gazing at the sunlit garden. "There's much that you don't know, my dear, and circumstances that are long in the past," he said quietly. "But I say don't judge your mother, for if she takes on the greater burden of care and it makes her rough, it may be my own fault for not lifting the burden myself."

Ann jumped up from her stool and threw her arms around her father. "You're a good man," she said, her voice muffled in his shirt.

"There, there," he said, giving her a pat.

With a smile for her, he put the cup back and left the shed. Ann finished the milking, and after taking the bucket into the house and down into the cellar, she returned to the byre to take Lace to pasture.

"Hot again today," Ann sighed, tapping the cow's tail with a switch. "I envy you sitting under a tree the whole day through and eating cool grass, I do."

Lace puffed loudly through her black nostrils and twitched her ears at the sound of Ann's voice. Together, girl and cow ambled through Marblehead to the fenced pasture the family owned outside of the town. Overhead the sky was already turning white with heat, and Ann waved flies away with the switch as she walked.

"There you are, you fine beast." When Ann gave the cow a slap on the rump, Lace trotted forward through the gate and immediately began tearing up mouthfuls of sweet grass. Ann slid home the rails that closed up the gate and leaned for a moment, watching the animal graze. She truly did envy Lace her luxury and dreaded the thought of going back to the inn. Her day would be filled, as usual, with cleaning and cooking and brewing and serving, and all in the heat that did not let up.

She wanted to escape. The scent of the ocean came to her on a faint breeze.

"Don't tell a soul where I'm off to," Ann said to

the cow. Lace flicked one ear her way, but continued to graze. With a glad, reckless laugh, Ann began running, not back toward town but toward the Neck, her blond hair coming loose from its knot and streaming out behind her.

At last she was out of breath and flushed with running, and her steps slowed. She trudged through the sand on the narrow spit that joined mainland to Neck, and then rambled over rocks, startling the sheep that pastured out there. On her right the ocean rolled away from her into an endless, shimmering haze, and there was no horizon. The tide was running out. A wet, raw, fishy smell, the smell of the brine, filled the air.

Ann sat down and leaned back against a sun-hot boulder. She shielded her eyes against the morning light, looking east, toward Scotland, and fancied that the air that cooled her had been cooled on Scotland's slopes. That land was a dream to her. Her grandfather, though native born to America, had told Bridie's tales of the old home country so often, that Ann could almost see it. Her friends had never understood why she felt as she did about that place. Reliance had always rolled her eyes and laughed when Ann mentioned Bridie MacKenzie.

A shadow passed through Ann as she remembered that this was the day that Reliance planned to run off. Would they go to England, or some other place? Ann wondered. Some years ago another Marblehead girl, a maid of the Fountain Inn named Agnes Surriage, had fallen in love with an Englishman, Sir Henry Frankland. He had wooed and won her, and Agnes had forsaken Marblehead forever. Of further details Ann knew only what gossip and rumor passed through the streets, the story embellished with new stitches each time a set of women bent over their needlework together. Agnes's name was spoken with scorn for it, and Ann was saddened to think that Reliance would be reviled, too.

But the soothing hush and lap of the combing waves drove those thoughts away, and she tipped her face to the white sky. Content, she emptied her mind and her spirit of its cares, and only dwelled on the luxury of a few moments alone with the ocean, the faroff crying of gulls, and the steady wind. This was the Marblehead she held dear, where obstinate rocks defied the sea and held off all intruders.

Dreaming, Ann turned her head. Her peace flew off in an instant. A young man was walking toward her.

Ann shrank back against the rock, keeping perfectly still. He was walking slowly, barefoot through the tidal pools, and his head was down. He carried something wet cradled in the tails of his shirt, and the cuffs of his white canvas breeches were rolled up to his knees.

Pass me by, she prayed silently. She hated to lose her scarce privacy. Holding her breath, she watched him come closer and closer. He still had not looked up but wore such an air of concentration as he stared down into the shallow puddles that Ann found herself wondering what fascinated him so. The light skimming over the water leaped up and dappled his downturned face, and his sea-bleached hair fell across his brow. Suddenly Ann realized she had forgotten to breathe and drew in a gulp of air with a loud gasp.

He looked up.

"Good day to you," he said.

Ann smiled ruefully. There was no way out of it, now. "Good day," she said with an air of finality.

"God amazes me."

"What's that?" Ann asked, surprised.

The young man climbed up the ledge to where she was, at ease and familiar. Ann could not believe he would be so forward as to join her. His smile was still absorbed, even as he knelt in front of her and tumbled out a load of black, glistening mussels onto the ground beside her. Ann raised her brows, more surprised all the time.

"See here," he said.

"Mussels?" Ann replied blankly.

"Amazing."

Ann edged slightly away, wondering why he did not heed her unwelcoming tone. "Mussels amaze you?"

He nodded and poked among the black, egg-shaped shells on the ground with one tanned finger. They were clamped tight shut and shining wet. "See how God protects the weak?" he said. "He gives the helpless things armor."

"And yet you plan to eat them, all the same," Ann said. "God cannot protect the mussel from you."

"Aye. God made man treacherous."

"You are a philosopher, I see," Ann said, still wishing he would go away.

The young man looked up at her with eyes the color of seawater, and he smiled disarmingly. "Being on the ocean makes a man so. I've never known such heapings of time when there's naught to do but think."

"You're a sailor, then, as well."

"A sailor and new to it," he said, "and still in awe of the wonders I see all around." He looked out at the ocean with a look of such bemused delight that Ann was intrigued in spite of herself.

"You weren't born to the sea? Few in Marblehead look at the ocean with anything but distrust. It is too perilous for us to admire it."

"No," he agreed. "I wasn't born to the sea, but to the farm."

Ann nodded. She knew the hard scratching life that the farmers of New England led, planting crops and harvesting rocks.

"You're not from these parts?" she ventured,

trying to place his accent among the many that she heard every day at the Wild Rose.

He waved his hand vaguely north and east but said nothing about it. Ann wondered if he meant Beverly or Salem, or even New Hampshire. She could hardly believe she was asking so many questions, when she was so often the one who must be dragged into conversation. But this young seafaring philosopher showed no wish to tease and flirt. Here was someone who cherished time as she did and did not waste it with pranks and boasts. She found it easeful and pleasant to know she need not speak if she did not want to.

And then she knew she did want to speak, to draw him out.

"They'll open in the pot," Ann said, nodding at the shellfish.

He looked up at her with such a smile that Ann had to smile back. "I won't be the one to betray them," he said, and in one swift motion hurled the lot of them back into the sea.

Ann stared, dumbfounded. "Why did you gather them, if not to eat them?" she asked.

"I don't know." He looked at her and let out a cheerful laugh. His blue-green eyes showed nothing but delight at his own foolishness, and his open, handsome face was lit with enjoyment. "But perhaps now they'll appreciate life and not lay about, clinging to rocks all day."

Ann let out a peal of laughter. "Maybe they'll become philosophers, too, and betake themselves to Harvard College."

"Maybe so. Do you know how to find clams?"

"Of course," Ann said, still laughing. "Come."

She clambered down from her perch, catching up a piece of driftwood as she went, and led the way down to the wet sand. The young sailor walked at her side, looking at the sky, the sea, the sand, and all with the same frank interest and enjoyment.

"What is your name?" she asked, too curious to resist.

"Roger," he replied. "And you?"

"Ann."

They smiled at one another. Ann's pulse suddenly began to race.

"Here," she said breathlessly, poking with her stick into the wet sand. For a moment she could not remember what she was meant to do. Then she composed herself. "Look for the bubbles."

"Bubbles?" Roger echoed.

Ann looked up at him and again could not think of a thing but how he looked and smiled and attended so calmly to her. "As the water goes out," she whispered.

With an effort she kicked off her shoes and kilted up her dress in one hand. Then she walked into the shallow, lapping waves. It was a relief how the water washed the heat from her skin.

"Now look down as the water goes out," she said, forcing herself to stop being foolish. Roger stood beside her, looking down. Ann stared at her bare feet and his in the shallow, moving water. Then beside her big toe, a stream of air bubbles rippled up. "Ah!" she gasped.

With furious concentration Ann began to dig where the bubbles were, her stick flinging up gobs of dripping sand. Then out popped a clam like a cherrystone plucked from a cherry.

"There it is." Roger stooped to retrieve the creature, which was already trying to bury itself again.

" 'Tis a simple thing," Ann said, wiping her forehead with one briny hand. She felt ridiculously pleased with herself for showing Roger how to dig clams and for doing it with such dispatch.

"Thank you." Roger handed the rough white shell to her.

"Thank you," Ann replied. Then, with a self-conscious smile, she tossed it into the combing waves.

Roger laughed. "And now you are a philosopher, too."

"Perhaps I am," Ann agreed, wiping her sticky salt-watery hand on her dress. "Though my thoughts are of interest to none but myself."

Roger tipped his head to one side. "I shouldn't be so sure of that," he said.

With a shy smile, Ann tossed her driftwood digger into the surf.

"Tell me," she said, eager to turn the talk away from herself. "You are the philosopher. What do you make of this quarrel between Crown and colonies?"

He squinted at the bright horizon. "I have had no education, and so my views are very simple. And yet from what I see, it seems to me a very plain thing."

"Plain? How?" Ann asked.

"As plain as a child growing to an adult," Roger said musingly. "When we are young, we are governed by our parents, who must know the best. But when we grow, we must think and decide for ourselves and not be led by others, and be prepared to change if circumstance requires. So it is with the colonies, I think. The colonies have outgrown their parents."

Ann looked at his profile. "It is simple, when you put it this way."

He gave her a quick smile. "Only a poor man's view, and so it must be simple. I think I must stay a sailor so I'll have time to complicate my thoughts."

"Life has enough complication in it," Ann said dryly. "So perhaps you must give up the sea and go back to farming."

"Perhaps." Roger looked out at the surf again and breathed deeply. "Isn't it good to have summer? Do you know that song, 'The Winter It Is Past'?"

Ann blushed and backed away, out of the water. "I may become a philosopher, but never a singer, I fear. I can't sing a note."

"Come, I'll never believe it," Roger said with a grin. "Only follow me."

"I can't, I say," Ann protested, laughing anyway.

"Oh the winter it is past, and the summer's come at last—" Roger sang in a fine, husky baritone that Ann could hear with her body. "And the small birds sing in every tree."

Ann put both hands over her mouth and shook her head.

"Come, follow it," Roger persisted. "Oh, the winter it is past—"

She shook her head in resignation, and the breeze flirted a strand of her blond hair across her eyes. "I've given you fair warning . . ." Drawing a deep breath, she repeated the line in such an off-key that Roger winced.

"You're playing," he said.

"I play not," Ann laughed, pulling the hair away from her face. "I did say I could not sing a note. I have no tricks in me."

"No," he said, his gaze lingering on her face. "I see that now."

She swallowed with some difficulty. She could not dissemble that she liked him. "Do you stay here long, in Marblehead port?" she asked shyly.

"I don't know." He turned away abruptly, a frown pulling his mouth down, and began to walk back to the rocks.

Puzzled and hurt, Ann watched him, her heartbeat pounding in her ears. The lightness had suddenly gone from the day.

Then Roger stopped and turned back to her. Ann's hopes instantly rose. "If you see me in the town, you may choose not to know me," he said.

"What? I don't understand."

He bent over to reach behind a boulder and then stood up. Ann's gaze dropped to his hand. He held a uniform jacket of the British Navy. The sand suddenly seemed to give way beneath Ann's feet, and she stared at him through tears of betrayal.

Quickly she scooped up her shoes and ran, stumbling back toward the town.

Chapter Five

"HOW DARE HE—impudent—I'll spit in his face—" Ann was fuming, muttering to herself as she toiled hotly up the dusty road into town. The sun seemed to drag at her heels and her hem, and puffs of dust rose from her footsteps like bursts of smoke. She could hardly see, so great was her anger and so hard was she stoking it. At the gate into the inn's garden, she fumbled with the catch. It stuck, and she beat at it, tears of anger filling her eyes.

"Damn—damn him," she whispered. She stopped and hung her head, feeling the sun's heat tighten its grip on the back of her neck. Hidden insects sawed monotonously in the heat in a steady, nagging whine.

Ann was ashamed of the tears that wet her cheeks and wiped them roughly away. She would not let a heartless English sailor prick her feelings, so instead she put aside the hurt and built upon the anger. She stared at the roses that grew in a tangle around the fence. They blazed passion red.

"I hate him," she said, lifting the catch of the gate.

She strode into the inn, stopping only to refresh herself with a short draught of ale in the kitchen. Coffee was boiling in a pot over the fire, and its sharp, acrid smell braced her. She snatched up a rag and went into the front room, where several men sat in the cool darkness, smoking up a lackadaisical conversation. They nodded at her as she entered, lifting their hands in greeting.

"Good day, Ann," said Mr. Braxton.

Ann bobbed her head and began polishing a pewter tankard. She spit on it and rubbed at it with the cloth until the metal gleamed like hot silver. There were two long shelves of pewter, enough to work out her temper, or so she hoped. By the closed shutters, the men's voices rose and fell. Snatches of their talk came to Ann but she did not heed them. Despite her best efforts, her mind played tricks with her, flashing up the image of Roger's face, and of a sleek black mussel shell shining on his open palm, and of the water-tossed light dancing across his tanned cheeks.

"Which of our ships is safe?" Mr. Devane complained, his voice sharp with indignation. "And which of our seamen safe from the British press gangs?"

Mr. Braxton snorted. "Remember you Michael Corbett? It was some years back, but when his *Pitt Packet* was boarded and Lieutenant Panton tried to kidnap him into the Navy, Michael barricaded himself below and swore to harpoon the officer."

"Aye, and so he did harpoon Panton," Mr. Devane said. "Spitted him like a lobster. Aye, I remember that well."

"Not a man is secure."

"Nor our females," spluttered Mr. Devane. "The British knaves sniff after them like the dogs they are."

Ann dropped her tankard, and it clanged like a bell on the hearthstone. The men turned their faces to her.

"Buttered your fingers again, Annie?" Mr. Braxton joked.

"Pray pardon, sirs," she said, her cheeks aflame. She bent to retrieve the mug. Her quick breath as she leaned over stirred the ashes in the hearth, sending them flying and swirling in a tiny tempest. She smelled the bite and tang of creosote.

"I tell you I'm sick of it," Devane continued, puffing smoke from his pipe like a chimney. "Is it not bad enough they've been traipsing around Boston for years, consorting with the daughters of that metropolis? But now they must poke and pry around here—and around our womenfolk!"

Braxton nodded judiciously, his long, lean face lined with disapproval. "And the worst of it is that some girls do return the same attention. In Boston, that is," he added.

"As if the lads bred in Massachusetts aren't good enough," complained a ship's caulker named Allston, a pockmarked, squint-eyed young man whom no girl had ever favored with a smile.

Devane flourished his pipe and pointed it at Braxton meaningfully. "It is not only Boston where the weaker nature of the female is shown by this unseemly attraction to the English. What of that Agnes? Eh? What of her?"

"Agnes Surriage, well—" Braxton mumbled into his ale, and shook his head in baffled resignation.

By the hearth, Ann carefully set down the last tankard and kept her face turned away.

"Well," Braxton said after a pause. "Well, that's done long in the past, it is, and Agnes perhaps not as wise as she should have been, or else more wicked. But I say today none of our Marblehead girls value our cause so paltry. The girls of Boston would do well to follow the example of our Ann here, or my Reliance."

He gave Ann a fatherly smile.

But she, in return, could only look down and twist her hands into her apron. Of Reliance he

72

would know only too soon. And like Agnes, Reliance would be scorned and reviled, her name abused throughout the town. This Ann knew, and her heart ached for her friend, and for Agnes, whose only crime was love.

For herself, however, she vowed she would not value her native land so paltry as to look pleasantly upon one of the tyrant's men. Roger had sought to trick her with gentle words for the American cause. But if she ever encountered him again, she would see only the open air and hear no voice but the voice of Marblehead.

With that resolution, Ann felt a heaving over of her heart, as of a boat lifted and set atoss on a sudden swell. She put her hand to her throat and felt the pulse tripping there. It was for gladness, she told herself—gladness that she knew where her course lay.

But she was frowning fiercely as she left the room.

Ann passed through into the hot, fire-lit kitchen, and in an instant a low murmur of voices broke off. She raised her eyes to see her brother and Nat Trelawney and Captain Carter sitting hunched at the table, their faces watchful in the stuffy silence.

"Ah, Ann," Carter said, relaxing in the next moment.

Her gaze traveled quickly from one to the other, from Carter's easy smile, to Nat's furtive, restless eyes, to John's grinning quietness. It was the quietness of a horse before it wheels around, or the calm of a wolf before it leaps forward, and by that quietness Ann was certain that they spoke of smuggling. She felt her heart sink. She knew this was sure confirmation that the adventurous Carter was in the thick of it.

"Captain Carter . . ." Ann sighed, going to the table. "Lead my brother out of this," she pleaded.

The men exchanged looks of amusement, and Captain Carter gently tapped her under the chin. "Now, Ann," he began.

"No, sir! I won't be coddled like a babe!" Ann broke in hotly and jerked her head from his touch. "I know what you do, and how you use John's youth and bravery!"

John laughed and poured ale into a mug from an earthenware pitcher. Drops of moisture trickled down the sides of the jug, wetting the table. "Annie, Annie," John chuckled, shaking his head and tracing one finger through the water. Nat grinned, showing his sharp teeth.

Ann stared at them, angry that they would endanger themselves so lightly. "There's righteousness in following the law—it matters not what law it is," she insisted as her brother snorted into his mug.

"If the rules and requirements wound our dignity, there is no dignity in obeying," Captain Carter spoke up. He put one elbow on the table and toyed with a knife that lay there. He dragged its point carelessly to and fro across the scarred tabletop. "Each time we take a prop from under their laws, their laws become weaker and weaker."

"And we cut the ropes that bind us to the king and his rascally Parliament strand by strand," John added.

Nat grinned sourly. "Aye, cutting is what's called for here. Cutting of ropes . . . And aught else."

Carter's knife stopped its restless movement, and Nat impetuously grabbed it and jabbed it down into the table. It quivered there, where the four of them stared at it in silence. Ann felt a coldness steal over her when she looked at Nat's face, and then a flush of fearful heat when she saw the glint in her brother's eyes. He welcomed it, he yearned for danger.

"Please. John."

"Now, then." Captain Carter turned from Ann, ignoring her entreaty. "Tonight, the Reverend Meacham will address a prayer for the health and complete good equipage of our militia. I trust you two will be gone from the house to listen?"

Ann blinked in confusion. "Prayer?"

"Ann," came her mother's voice. "Don't ask questions you won't like the answering of."

Mistress MacKenzie came into the kitchen with a plucked chicken by the neck. She put it down on

75

the table, and began gutting it in businesslike fashion. Her fingers were soon covered with blood. Ann felt sickened and felt an awful pressure behind her ribs. Too many people around her were filled with secret knowledge, too many people had knives at the ready. The blade that cut and carved in her mother's hand glinted dully in the light of the fire. One of the cats slunk in and licked drops of blood from the floor.

"Does my father go to hear this prayer as well?" Ann asked in a high, unnatural voice.

"My father is godly enough," John murmured, meeting Ann's eyes steadily. "I think you won't mention it to him."

Ann swallowed hard and looked at the others. Those she knew well were suddenly strangers to her, and the familiar kitchen, with blackened beams stretching across the ceiling, the iron crane in the hearth, the battered benches and dough box—all, all seemed different, shifted into new and sinister poses. The men at the table met Ann's baffled anger with silence, scratching in the tabletop with the sides of their thumbnails or rubbing their chins or gazing at the fire. The room was stifling hot and stank of chicken blood and scalding coffee.

"You think my father would betray his son?" Ann spoke into the silence at last.

"Nay, Ann! What a thought!" Captain Carter put his head back and laughed heartily. "There's never a better, kinder man in the Massachusetts Colony than Matthew MacKenzie, and he loves John as he loves his life."

Ann's mother nodded silently, still gutting the bird and throwing the giblets on the floor where the cat gnawed at them with finicking savageness. John leaned across the table, reaching for Ann's hand. She let him hold it, but did not return the pressure of his fingers on hers.

"Ann, our father would only be grieved to know where the kegs come from, for he'd feel his duty to protect us all." John spoke quietly, but emphatically, and as he spoke Ann tried to pull her hand from his, but he held tight. "Do not speak of this to him. 'Tis for his own sake and safety."

Then Ann did wrench her hand from his hard grasp. She was hurt and ashamed for her father that they valued him so low. They treated him as they treated a child. She flushed and felt the sting of strong resentment toward Captain Carter. She saw her mother look at him also and felt her anger flare hotter.

"You should have married him, Mother," Ann blurted out, flinging one hand toward the handsome seaman. "He's a man of action. He's the very picture of a romantic fellow."

Her mother met her look with silence and then let out a bitter laugh. "Romantic? That's where you recommend marriage? That, my girl, will break your heart. I was not such a fool." With another dry sniff, she tossed the chicken into a pot that hung from the crane in the fire. The sizzle was shockingly loud.

John broke the awkward silence with a laugh. "I didn't know you had a heart to be wary of, Mother."

"Maybe I had once, you unnatural child." Mistress MacKenzie wiped her hands on her apron, her eyes stormy as she looked at her former suitor.

Captain Carter released a long sigh. "Ah, well," he said, clapping his hands to his knees and rising. "I must be to my ship. I'll see you mates this evening."

"Listening to the Reverend Mr. Meacham," John said, his eyes sparkling. Mistress MacKenzie poked at the chicken, which sizzled louder.

"Oh, go to your cursed prayer service and I hope you choke on it," Ann shouted at her brother.

She turned on her heel and fled out the back door and into the garden with its bright hum of bees. At first she was blinded by the glare and stood there, full of fear and frustration. Everyone and everything around her was ready to war, it seemed, and decisions of a terrible weight were being made on every side. Was she the only one in her circle whose heart was not hard and braced for battle? she wondered.

"When did this happen, this change of things?" she whispered.

"Change of what things, child?"

Her father's voice startled her. Ann turned and saw him sitting on a stone in the shadow of the tavern, quietly smoking a pipe. At once the clutch of fear and doubt left her. With a sigh, Ann sat at his feet and rested her cheek against his knee.

"You look so tired, Ann," he said, caressing her hair. "What troubles you?"

"Everything," she replied.

"The world is a troublesome place, that's true." Mr. MacKenzie puffed in silence for a moment and then tapped out the embers on a stone. "I've just now loaded three barrels of our salt cod onto Braxton's wagon so that he may take it to the wanting folk of Boston. With their port closed and trade at a halt, they have troubles indeed, poor souls."

"Yes, they do, Father," Ann said distractedly.

Her father patted her head again. "Now, won't you tell me what hurts you, my girl?"

Ann raised her eyes to his kind, familiar face. He was surely not a romantic man. Stood beside Captain Carter, he would appear only pale and timid. But he was generous and good and stalwart. Ann felt a prick of indignation again that the others kept him ignorant.

"Father," she began, searching his face for some sign that he felt the same. "Don't you sometimes wish to take over more of the managing of this place? It is your tavern, from grandfather and from his father."

He smiled at her, and his blue eyes twinkled. "Your mother wouldn't care to have me poking into things. She has the running of the place and does it admirably well, better than I could do and keep it ready for John."

"But, Father!" Ann pushed herself away and stood to look down at him. She wanted to tell him, to shake him, to shout at him that his wife and son were in league with smugglers, that the rum he served so genially was traded at great cost.

But he only took her hand and smoothed her fingers. "Ann, things are not always what they seem," he said in a low voice.

Ann felt her fingertips prickle with alarm. "What—what do you mean?"

"Only that we all have parts to play. You see mine, and I am content to play it." He met her eyes squarely, and in his look Ann read love and knowledge and pity. He knew all, it seemed. All.

"Father." Ann shook her head. She was terribly bewildered. "Why?"

"I am willing to purchase peace in my home," he said with a tender smile. "It is no real cost to me."

"No cost but your honor," Ann whispered.

She instantly regretted her words, but Mr. MacKenzie frowned thoughtfully. "Honor is something I can well do without," he told her. "It has no value to me."

"It does to John."

"Aye, it does to John, but he's young." Her father stretched his arms above his head and smiled sadly. "As for me, I'm happy to be a simple man, exciting no one's jealousy or suspicions, and in return I have this place preserved. I was born here, as my father was, and you twins also. I look ahead, and I know that the Wild Rose will be here for John to carry on with when I'm gone."

Ann sat down beside him again. "And so will I carry on here."

"No, no, darling. You'll be married off to one of these fine fellows in the town, settled into a steady life with a family of your own," her father said.

Ann twined her fingers through his, her thoughts revolving wearily in her head. Judith, Reliance, and her mother: these three women showed too clearly what love and marriage might mean. For Judith, loving reckless John MacKenzie would undoubtedly bring her grief; Reliance Braxton was going to orphan herself for love of a British sailor; and Ann's mother had thrown passion away with both hands and taken bad temper as her portion. Love and marry and settle into a steady life? Ann asked herself as she looked at the herbs of the garden.

"No, I do not believe so," she said, her gaze lingering over a patch of rue and the sad-scented thyme. "I do not believe I will ever marry. I do not wish it."

"But, my dear," her father began.

Ann stood up quickly, shaking her head with a smile to hide the tears that were in her eyes. Life in Marblehead had always seemed sweet and easy. But this summer it was filled only with a heavy heat.

She walked slowly to the lush tangle of the roses that twined along the fence and up the side of the house. Bridie had planted the roses long ago, and the blooms had always been a joy to Ann, and a remembrance. Standing by them now, Ann looked at the blood red flowers and saw only a scarlet warning.

Evening found Ann restless and on edge, and regretful of the angry words she had flung at her brother. She had not seen him since she'd run from the kitchen into the hot afternoon.

Now the sun had set in a steamy haze behind the town, and windows up and down the length of Front Street were open to the evening air. The tavern was filled with men seeking relief from the heat and their heavy cares. Ann carried mugs of ale and cider and rum, wiping her forehead with her apron, her eyes stinging in the tobacco smoke. Each time the door opened, she looked for John to come in. But she knew he would not. He and his mates had a serious errand, as she knew only too well.

"Allender not here, this evening," Mr. Pearson said as Ann placed a tankard before him. "That's as welcome as a sup of beer."

Ann glanced over her shoulder. For once the room was free of British sailors and officers, and to Ann their absence spoke loud. Her throat worked dryly. She looked again, slowly, searching each face, but not a king's man was in the place.

"John," she whispered.

"Eh?" Mr. Pearson cupped one hand to his hairy ear.

Without answering, Ann hastened out of the room. She stepped out the front door into the street, swerving to avoid a trio of drunken fishermen singing bawdily as they lurched along. Swiftly, more swiftly, Ann walked and then ran through the town to the bluffs overlooking the water.

The night was black around her, and the ocean black, too. Ann tripped over a rock, regained her balance, and went cautiously forward, sensing the void ahead at the edge of the cliff. John was in danger. Ann knew this by instinct, as she had always known since they were children when her twin was hurt or threatened.

Now instinct told her that he was down there, down on the black water. Ann fought to control her breathing and walked quickly while the wind whipped her skirt around her legs. She kept watch over the ocean that conveyed John on his task and above her, in the quadrant of Perseus, meteors flashed, and flashed again, and coursed blazing streaks through the sky.

Ann stared at them, taking no joy in their distant beauty. She only saw that the stars were dying. One after the other streaked across the heavens, glorying in its fiercest light as it burned out. Heavy-hearted, Ann followed the path of one blazing bright star as it fell into the sea and disappeared. Where it fell, a shadow moved on the water. Her heart clenched within her.

The shadow resolved itself into a silent, stealing schooner, slipping out from cover of the Neck. If the sun were to rise and shine forth, it would only tell Ann what she already knew for certain. That schooner was Allender's ship, *Southampton*.

And somewhere below Ann's outlook, rocking on the tide, was her brother, awaiting a signal that would bring Allender down on him like a hurricane. She leaned against the wind.

"JOHN!"

The wind snatched the call from her mouth, and the next moment Ann had grabbed up her skirts and begun scrambling diagonally down the rocks, heading for the sandy beach. In the darkness she stumbled and slipped, falling onto her hands. Grit and sharp shingle drove into her palms. The wind filled her ears, and her heart rioted with a terrible fear.

"John, don't go, don't signal," she gasped, plunging ever downward. Her dress snagged on a rock, and she yanked at it. A few more steps and she fell the last few feet onto the level ground. She began to run in earnest.

"John!"

Then a light flickered once, twice, out on the smooth, gleaming water, and was answered by another close to shore. And then there was a crack and hiss, and the night was lit by flares streaming down more brightly than the stars ever could. Ann stopped on the beach, blinking, and saw her brother and Nat and their small boat making wildly for shore, and in the next instant came the boom of a cannon, followed by the splash and hiss of steam as a ball plunged into the ocean. The rattling snap of musket fire clattered like a snare drum and then the flares, like meteors, plummeted into the waves and went out.

Chapter Six

ANN'S FEET SANK in the sand as she struggled to find her brother in the sudden darkness. Shots continued to crack from the *Southampton*, kicking up and ricocheting from the black waves. "John! Where are you?"

"Here!" Nat's voice came to her.

Ann followed the sounds of splashing and toiling in the water and stumbled to the surf's edge. "Where?" she demanded, straining to hear over the racket of musketfire. Wakened shorebirds shrieked and scattered on all sides, blundering madly past Ann in the darkness, out to sea. She heard someone slogging and churning through the shallow water toward her.

"Here I am," John gasped, his voice strained. "We have guests."

"John, I tried to stop—"

"I know," John cut her off. Nat was heaving and dragging the dinghy onto the beach, cursing furiously in a steady, poisonous stream under his breath as he plowed it through the wet heavy sand. John groped for Ann's hand. He gripped it very tightly, his own hand dripping. "I am glad you're here, Ann. Come, hurry."

But Ann dug in her heels. "What's wrong? Tell me, I know something's wrong with you!"

"Annie," he said, his voice both laughing and warning. "Your love for argumentation is a little overstrong. We're being shot at. Hurry!"

Ann ran with him, kicking up sand behind her as she raced. At first John kept up with her, but very quickly his steps began to falter. He panted at her side and once fell heavily against her. Nat led the way.

"They'll be putting to shore in longboats," Nat muttered as the musketfire ceased. "They'll soon be on us."

"Get me back to the Rose," John said.

He stopped for a moment's rest before climbing the steep path. His breath came in uneven gasps, and his face in the faint starlight gleamed with seawater and sweat. Ann put one arm around his waist to help him, fearing to know what had happened.

"You're hurt?" she whispered. She rubbed her fingers together. They were slick.

"Me?" John laughed, and then stifled a curse as

87

they began a hasty scramble. They still had a far distance to go, but lights beckoned from ahead.

"Just a little way," Ann said, her gaze darting from shadow to shadow. Her brother was heavy against her, and she pulled him, growing tired herself. The way seemed uncommonly long, and each stone and hole in the road threatened to topple them. John grunted with each step.

At last they were among the houses. Ann willed herself to be strong and not think of how often her brother stumbled. She must get him home. "Here we are at Front Street."

"Home, my home, my loving home," John sang unevenly. He caught his breath. "Damn them."

Ann caught the glint of Nat's eyes as they passed a lighted window. Nat narrowed his gaze and took John's elbow to help him along. Ann shuddered. Nat—and Carter—had a heavy reckoning to make for coaxing John into such danger.

"Here's home," she whispered thankfully, seeing the Wild Rose Inn up ahead. Welcome light and sound poured forth from the open door, and men stood there with their tankards and pipes, lit from behind, smoking in the open air and laughing. Never had it looked better to her.

"To the back." Nat steered them down an alley, and came to the back fence of their garden, near Lace's shed. "Up, John."

John grabbed the fence with both hands, swung

one leg up, and then tumbled over as his arm buckled.

"John—" Ann bit off her cry, clutching empty air.

"I'm well enough," her brother said, on his knees on the grass. "Help me up."

Her hands shaking, Ann pulled herself awkwardly over the fence, plucking her skirt free when it caught. She leaned over to help John stand. "Where is your wound?" she asked.

"My shoulder."

Nat ran stealthily ahead in the shadows to the back door. Ann stood at her brother's side, hearing his painful breathing, feeling her own shoulder begin to ache. She could not keep her arms from trembling, and so hugged them around herself. Her mind was empty but for one thought that repeated itself. John is shot. John is shot.

Beside her, John leaned on the fence, panting, and throwing out an occasional violent oath against the British sailors. He was furious, and in pain.

Nat paused on the stone step and cautiously opened the door. The red firelight from within streamed out and lit up one side of his narrow face like a goblin mask before he turned and waved them on.

"Now," Ann whispered hoarsely, sliding her arm again around her brother's waist. In step, they hurried across the dark garden and over the sill. Ann helped him over the doorstep, and he fell the rest of the way into the kitchen, catching himself against the broad table.

Their mother came swiftly to his side, her mouth set in a stern line. "Get him upstairs, quick," she said to Ann.

Ann stood where she was, seeing for the first time the shocking red stain that had spread across the white cambric of John's shirt. Even as she watched, it crept further across the cloth. Her face drained of color.

"I reckon the ball went clear through," Nat muttered, poking and prodding at John's shoulder with hard, nimble fingers. John winced and went pale, but said nothing.

"Patch him up, Ann. Hide him. And you, Nat Trelawney. Make yourself scarce." Mistress MacKenzie noticed Ann's rigid posture and shook her elbow. "Look sharp! You're no good to him this way. And change your clothes. You're bloody."

Ann blinked, and the room and all its contents came into her sight again. She saw the sleeve of her chemise was bright crimson, and it stuck wetly to her skin. Plucking at the bloody cloth, Ann moved to her brother's side again, and then all froze. A tumult and commotion reached them from the front of the tavern, and rough commands sounded through the closed doors.

"Allender." Ann grabbed John's hand and

dragged him out of the kitchen, down the corridor to the empty parlor. She flung open the door of the closeted stairs, and they plunged upward into the darkness. The silent walls of their house closed protectively around them.

"The small attic," Ann whispered, feeling her brother's weight grow heavier against her arm. His breath rasped in her ear. "You must hide in there."

They could not lighten their footsteps as they ran down the corridor. Ann groped in the dark for the door of her own room. Under the eaves, a blanket box stood before a trapdoor, where the space between the old house and an addition was used for storage. Feeling her way blindly, she knelt down and heaved at the box with all her strength.

"I can't move it," she gasped. She heard Allender's voice raised below, and her heartbeat skipped wildly.

"Let me." John knelt by her and put his weight to the task, but then grunted and slumped.

Ann tried to collect herself. The hurried tread of booted feet sounded from every side, it seemed, keeping step with the pulse that raced in her ears.

"Come," she said, hauling her brother up as she stood. She half led, half hoisted John onto the bedstead.

"Oh, God," he groaned. "My oath."

"Quiet." Ann put one hand gently over his

mouth. She felt his lips tremble against her fingers. Their breathing was harsh in the dark, hot room, and they both listened, straining.

"Go see," John whispered urgently. "See what is happening."

Ann bit her lip. "Do you still bleed?"

John did not answer. Ann fumbled at the bed-clothes and then yanked at the sheet with both hands until it came away. She wadded a corner of it.

"Hold this to your wound if you've strength enough," she whispered, pressing it against John's shoulder.

His hand came up and covered it. He cleared his throat. "Good."

Ann's fingers shook as she struggled with the buttons of her dress. She yanked her blood-soaked chemise over her head, balling it and stuffing it under the bed. In the dark, she found a clean chemise by touch and drew it on, tucking it awkwardly down inside her dress and fingering the buttons of the bodice into place.

With the caution and stealth of fear, Ann slipped out of the room and crept down the front stairs to the tavern. At the foot of the stairs was a plank door that did little to quell the usual rise and fall of voices on busy nights. But this night a guarded silence lay behind the door. There was only the clipped and commanding note of Allender's voice. Ann paused on the last step to steady herself. She knew she must wear an everyday face if her brother was to go unmolested.

Then she cracked the door and looked out, and her eyes immediately met Roger's. He stood with the regiment, musket at his shoulder. Her stomach made a vicious twist, and she jerked backward.

"Where have you been this night?" Allender demanded of Mr. MacKenzie.

Ann's father spread his hands wide, and he smiled, though his eyes were troubled. "Here, Captain Allender, serving my guests."

"And where else would he be?" Mistress MacKenzie asked. She strode forward to stand at her husband's side. Her eyes were cold and defiant.

Captain Allender swept back the tails of his coat and clasped his hands behind him. He surveyed the room with a haughty gaze, and every Marbleheader there returned his look with hatred. At the hearth, an old fisherman named Stubbs hawked and spat into the dead ashes. The midshipmen and sailors of Allender's company shifted their feet and changed grips on their muskets as the silence stretched tighter. Ann looked at each weapon in amazement, thinking she must see some sign, some indication of which one had shot her brother. She did not look at Roger's.

Allender suddenly turned on his heel and

pulled out a chair to sit on. "My men will search this place stem to stern," he announced.

"And for what?" Mr. MacKenzie asked.

"Contraband. We have information that smuggled liquors have been carried here."

Ann looked swiftly at her mother. Such illegal stuffs and stores as they had must be safely stowed away or off the premises entirely, for Mistress MacKenzie only made a disdainful shrug.

"Search all you like," the woman said. "And if you find my shirking daughter, tell her to come down and work. She hides in her room like a cowering calf."

Ann marveled at her mother's coolness. At the same time, she also itched at her mother's willingness to call ridicule on her. It was an excuse for Ann's absence, but it galled. She squared her shoulders and stepped down into the tavern.

"Here I am, Mother."

All eyes turned to her. Allender smiled. "Ah, Ann. We've missed your company."

"I hide from unwelcome advances, Captain," Ann said, stressing the last word. A ripple of uneasy laughter greeted this, and there was a stirring among the local men.

Ann's mother crossed to her quickly and turned her by the elbow. "Light the candles upstairs," she said in a loud voice, and then, so softly that only

Ann could hear, "You've still blood on your apron. Go." Thrusting a betty lamp into Ann's hand, Mistress MacKenzie shooed Ann up the steps and shut the door with a bang that echoed in the stairwell.

Behind her, Ann heard Allender barking out orders. "Search the cellars and the attics especially. This place is a rabbit warren of hiding places. Tell me if you find the young MacKenzie."

Ann hurried back to her room, the light flickering and wavering before her, and untied her apron with one hand. When she entered the chamber, John was once more kneeling beside the chest that hid the attic door. He was as pale as the moon, his face shining with sweat.

"No time," Ann warned, even as she heard the first of Allender's men tramping up the stairs. She helped her brother back to the bed and shook out a coverlet, and was about to draw it up over his wound when the door opened. Roger entered, ducking his head through the low doorway. Ann froze.

Roger looked at her, and at John and the red-stained sheet. A frown creased his brow. Ann heard blood pound in her ears. The silence in the small, hot room was terrible, and the wan light of the betty lamp wavered over them all, throwing strange shadows across the walls and ceiling.

"What news?" came a shout.

Roger raised his eyes to Ann. Staring at him, Ann slowly shook her head. The silence grew hotter.

Then Roger moved. "It is the girl's chamber," he called over his shoulder.

Ann was aware of a sudden stillness in her brother, and she knew he stared at her. But she could not look away from Roger. Without another word, the young sailor left.

"Who is he?" John hissed as she finished covering him up. He plucked weakly at the blanket but his eyes were hard. "Do you know him?"

"I—I—" Ann pressed her hands together. Outside the room, the other sailors were ransacking the place, flinging open doors, rummaging through boxes. She heard derisive mocking laughter and low, muttered abuse, heard the crash of a small table knocked over. Her face burned with anger and fear. Her house was being molested.

"What is he to you?" John asked again. Ann shook her head and made a cutting motion with her hand. She was trying to listen.

"Was anyone in that chamber?" a rough voice asked out in the corridor.

There was a pause, and then Roger replied. "It was only—"

Before he could finish, a lieutenant shouldered his way into the room, two other sailors at his heels and Roger, expressionless, bringing up the rear.

The lieutenant, a broad-shouldered, round-faced man with small eyes, stared boldly at Ann, and then looked at Roger. "And what doings have we here?" He grinned lewdly, nudging Roger in the ribs with one bulky elbow. "Thought you'd keep this discovery to yourself, eh? A pretty girl and a bed."

Roger stared past the lieutenant's shoulder. "And the brother, Lieutenant," he added.

"Eh?" The officer noticed John for the first time, covered up to the chin in bedclothes. He scowled and stepped nearer.

Ann was terrified, but her mind was very clear. "He's drunk," she said in a loud, steady voice. John, instantly taking her meaning, began to sing and babble.

"My love is like the red red nose," he slurred. Then he giggled and pulled the covers up past his eyes.

Ann gave the bedstead a kick. "He's a drunken fool for falling into the harbor and cracking his head. And I'm stuck mending him."

One of the sailors guffawed and clapped his mate on the back. "These 'Headers fancy theyselves such mariners, but can't keep from toppling off the wharf!"

"We'll question him downstairs," the lieutenant said.

John's singing rose in pitch from under the covers, and Ann kicked the bed again. She knew if he was taken his wound would be discovered. "He'll only be sick on your boots," she said.

"Haven't we enough to do with drunken colonists?" Roger spoke up in a bored voice. "Sir, there's no profit in this. There's still rooms to be searched and this fool was up to nothing worse than sousing himself this night. If we arrested every drunkard in Marblehead we'd empty the town."

"Perhaps," the lieutenant said. He shifted his piggish gaze from John to Ann, and began to smile. He took two steps closer to her, and she held her breath to avoid smelling him. His shadow reared up grotesquely behind him. "If this maid gives us some assurances, some bond that her brother—"

"I'd rather she gave us some beer," Roger said.

Ann let her breath out as the officer moved away from her. "Aye." He gave the bed a savage kick of his own as he passed. "What a parcel of pitiful specimens this land yields. Now, girl, we'll trouble you for a drink and a smile."

Clenching her jaw, Ann picked up the lamp and walked past the men. She felt their eyes on her as she led the way down the corridor. She heard coarse laughter and could well imagine them exchanging winks and bawdy grins. But not Roger. He would not love such sport, she was sure.

Then Ann scolded herself for speculating and

hurried her pace. He was no different from the others, but had some deep purpose of his own for what he did. Now she only wanted as much distance between herself and them as possible, and she ran down the stairs to the tavern.

The moment she entered, she felt danger. Captain Carter had arrived in her absence and now sat at his ease across a table from Allender, smiling pleasantly.

"Let me stand you a drink, sir," Carter said.

Allender smiled also, but it was not so pleasant. "Thank you, no. I still have unfinished business to attend. But I'll say I notice you spend much time here."

"Ah, I'm guilty." Captain Carter shrugged. "I haunt this place for the sake of an old love—and a new one." He held up a tumbler of rum and winked.

Ann stood rigid. She looked at her mother, who gazed from one captain to the other, and then to her husband. All three knew that Allender would not be appeased. He had come close to his prey this night and would not leave the chase.

"And did you find the young pup?" Allender asked the lieutenant.

"Drunk as a rigger," came the reply. "If there was ever any liquor, he's swallowed it all."

Ann couldn't help glancing at Roger. She did not know why he had hidden the truth, and so could not trust that he would keep it hidden. But no matter what Roger did, Allender still might decide to haul John out of bed. She turned pleading eyes to Captain Carter, whose fault this was.

"Let's pour some fine Canary wine for my fellow captain," Carter insisted jovially, clapping one hand down on the table with a bang. "We'll have him dancing a hornpipe yet. He'll soon see that we have nothing in *this* world to hide, and so may go and seek for it in the next with my blessings."

Allender stood up and spoke in a quiet voice to his men. "Arrest him," he said, pointing at Captain Carter.

"No!" Ann stepped forward.

"Ann," her mother warned.

Allender turned, arching his brows, and walked toward Ann. He circled her slowly. "And again you come to protect this man? What an avenging angel you are, Ann, so hot, so fierce. You should direct that passion elsewhere." He stopped behind her and leaned close to speak into her ear. "You are fierce, Ann. And delightful."

Ann stood ramrod straight, staring into space. She could feel his breath on her cheek. Everyone in the room waited. She wanted to kill him.

"Sir, this lady is frightened."

It was Roger who spoke, and all eyes turned to him. Allender slowly straightened. His face went pale with anger as he glared at Roger. "Sailor, I gave an order to arrest that pirate there. Carry it out."

Scowling, Allender picked up his tricorne hat from the table and strode out of the inn, followed closely by the lieutenant. Roger and two other sailors took Captain Carter's arms and led him away. At the door, Roger glanced quickly back at Ann, then turned and went out. The rest of the regiment followed.

In an instant the tavern was awash in outraged speculation and complaint, and the men jumped from their seats and gestured angrily to one another as they talked. Ann stood where she was as the current of political clamor raged around her, and she wondered at what had happened.

Then her legs began to tremble, and there was a ringing in her ears. Ann stumbled into the kitchen, trying to battle the faintness that was drowning her.

"God save us," she whispered, groping for a chair by the hearth. "When will they leave us alone?"

Mistress MacKenzie stood facing the fire, both hands on the mantel. As Ann regained her strength, she looked up at her mother and was shocked to see tears glistening in the firelight. In all her life, Ann had never seen her mother cry.

"Mother?"

"No span of time will ever be great enough,"

Mistress MacKenzie whispered, staring at the flames. "There will never be a time when that man has no power to hurt me."

"Who do you mean? Is it Allender?"

"Allender?" Mistress MacKenzie sneered, wiping her face roughly with the back of one hand. "Nay, not him, but that devil Carter."

"You speak as though you hate him," Ann said, more frightened and amazed at each word her mother spoke.

"Perhaps I do."

Ann was bewildered. The fire sent up a sudden shower of sparks beside her, and her entire body trembled from the tension of the night's doings, and she feared it was about to become even worse. "Mother, I don't understand—"

"No, you don't, do you?" Mistress MacKenzie turned on her quickly. "Things are not so simple as you always wish them to be, Ann. You are angry when you are treated as a child, yet you will not leave off behaving as one. Shall I tell you the truth? Do you truly wish to understand?"

Speechless, Ann stared at her mother. She was afraid, and wanted to shout for her mother to stop. But she could not speak.

"I was wild and willful at the age you are now," her mother said, fixing Ann with her eyes. "And I gave myself to Carter because I thought I could compel him to marry me. And then he went off to sea, and I was with child and no way to get him back."

"No." Ann shook her head. The world seemed to spin around her.

"And there was Matthew MacKenzie, faithful as ever, and willing to take me."

"Did he know?" Ann whispered. "Did you tell him?"

Her mother's eyes glinted. "Do you think I wouldn't honor him even that much?" she said through gritted teeth. "Yes, he knew, and still would have me. And so we married, and that baby died."

Ann covered her face with her hands. "Oh, God," she cried, tears seeping through her fingers. "Please. Don't tell me."

"And Carter comes back again and again, and tries to take my son from me, and yet I would sooner die than never see that man again because for all that I still love him. If John dies I'll still love Carter."

"Don't tell me any more," Ann pleaded. Her fingers clenched in her hair. She shook her head from side to side in her lap, crying. She wanted to make everything stop, make the tide cease rushing from her.

Her mother let out her breath in a shuddering sigh. "Ann, the world is not what you thought it was, and never was nor ever will be."

"Mother," Ann choked. She raised her tear-streaked face, hurt and afraid. "What's to become of us?"

Mistress MacKenzie pushed a burnt log-end back into the fire with the toe of her shoe. "I don't know, Ann. See to your own sails and halyards. That is all you can do."

Chapter Seven

ANN LOOKED IN on her brother in the morning, saw him asleep, and so went out to the shed to milk Lace. When she returned to the kitchen, she found her mother preparing a poultice for him. Ann felt herself flush hot and then cold as she met her mother's eyes. Mistress MacKenzie looked at her forbiddingly, and Ann knew she would speak of what had passed between them last night at her own peril.

"Take this to your brother," Mistress MacKenzie said curtly, holding out the medicine-soaked compress.

Ann hesitated. "Mother, I—"

"Take it."

Her mother left the room abruptly. With a sigh, Ann took the poultice and climbed the stairs.

In John's room, Ann found Judith at his bedside, and John awake though pale.

"You look as well as ever, more than you've a right to," Ann said. She leaned close and pressed her cheek to his. "I do thank God," she whispered.

"No. Thanks to you, Ann. And now you see I have a red-haired nurse," John said, rousing himself with a wan smile.

Ann stood and leaned in the doorframe, fanning herself with one hand. She gave her friend a look of gratitude as Judith applied the compress to John's shoulder. "How is your patient?" she asked.

"Lucky to be alive," Judith replied, her eyes flashing. "Those murderous British nearly had his heart with that bullet."

"Ah, but they didn't get it, for someone else has a prior claim." John's eyes were on Judith, and she turned pink with pleasure.

Over Judith's head, Ann asked John a silent question. How much did Judith know? John shook his head slightly, and Judith caught their exchange.

"He won't tell me a thing," the girl said with a pout. Her voice was bright, but she was clearly masking her fear over John's plight. "He *says* it was only an accident, that a musket misfired at him in the militia's training ground."

John grinned and shrugged, and then winced at the pain in his shoulder. "That is what I said, yes."

"I don't believe it for a moment." Judith stood

up and crossed the room, her skirts swishing in her agitation. Two bright spots of color burned in her cheeks. She was dangerously close to tears.

From the door Ann watched silently. She wished that Judith did know all, and that she could talk with her friend over what Roger had done. He had seen the bullet wound on her brother, and any British sailor abroad last night knew it was smugglers under fire in the dark. Any fool could draw the right conclusion. And yet Roger had said nothing. Ann burned to know why.

She watched, biting her lip, as Judith wrapped clean bandages around John's wound. For all his smiles and careless manner, he had lost much blood, and his face was pale and drawn under his deep tan. The bullet had missed his heart, perhaps, but had still done its damage. It remained to be seen if the wound festered.

"I have work," Ann said, pushing herself wearily upright. "Call to me, John, if you require me."

"I will."

"Annie, hold a moment." Judith followed her into the passage, where dust motes floated gently in a shaft of sunlight. Judith led Ann by the elbow to the window, and they stood there with their heads together.

"Last night Reliance was caught absconding with a British sailor," Judith said softly.

107

Ann's eyes filled and her vision swam. "Oh, no. Then they did not escape."

"You knew?" Judith gaped at Ann. "You knew of Reliance's elopement with this—this *Englishman*?"

"Yes." Ann turned to the window and looked out on the higgledy-piggledy maze of streets that twisted up and back from the tavern, the houses perched like so many gulls on outcroppings of rock, facing every which way with fussy obstinacy. Above, the sky was a clear, high blue, the clouds hurrying out to sea.

"Oh, Reliance," she whispered. "Whom can you rely on now?"

Judith tossed her head. "It's a disgrace, and Reliance has shamed us all by what she did. Falling in love with the enemy!"

"But—" Ann turned away from the window and looked unhappily at her friend. "But you said only the other day that country must not be a bar to loving. Now you say the heart practices politics, too?"

"Don't throw my words back at me when John lies wounded of an English bullet," Judith retorted, but her face colored in embarrassment. She made a petulant movement with one hand, and then looked away. "I know I said that."

"But you did not mean it?" Ann asked.

A tear rolled down Judith's cheek. "I do not know what I mean. But I know they tried to kill John. And today that is all I know."

Ann put her arm around Judith's shoulders, and they rested their heads together, both their hearts hurting for John's sake. Ann felt a terrible sadness take hold of her. The world seemed a hard hard place, and each day brought new woes.

"What will become of Reliance and her English lover?" she asked, gazing out the window beside her friend.

"Reliance is banished to Connecticut, where the Braxtons have kin. She is already gone," Judith answered, her voice a halting murmur. "And her lover is to be hanged for desertion."

Then, with a shudder, Judith began to cry, and Ann cried, too: for John, for Reliance, for her friend's doomed lover, and for them all.

Later, when Ann had taken Lace to pasture, she made her way to the harbor. She wanted to believe her concern was to get word of Captain Carter, since her brother's fate was close-linked with the captain's. In her heart, however, she knew she wished to see Roger, to ask an explanation from him. But she made Captain Carter's safety her only object.

The harbor was awash with mariners, merchants, and officials, their shouts ringing out, each one clamoring with the gulls to yell the loudest. Men trundled barrows filled with stores and wares, and mules hitched to wagons switched their tails at the goading flies. Halyards snapped against masts, barrels rumbled down gangways, block and tackle creaked and squealed. A dog ran in frenzied circles, barking for no reason, until someone kicked it into the water. A high-bred horse was led prancing and sidestepping up a gangway by an Indian, a length of sacking wrapped around its tossing head to cover its eyes. At the top, as it gained the deck, it lashed out with its rear hooves, raising a howling storm of curses from a pig-tailed seaman.

And on every side were trades and tirades, deals and disagreements. Men waved their arms and slapped sheaves of paper against their palms with ardent oaths. One merchant, whose tricorne hat was so limp and worn that its flaps hung down on each side, was so irate as to stamp his feet in fury and dash a leather case full of papers into the harbor, screaming at an official. Ann winced at the constant rage and rancor. She waved impatiently at the flies that hovered around, and searched the crowd of ships for Captain Carter's *Valor*. There were British sailors scattered throughout the throng, each with a clear pool free of colonists moving with him, as the native seamen gave the king's men a wide berth.

A boy Ann knew who shipped with Carter slouched by, a bucket of tar in each hand.

"Arch!" she called. "Archbald Dixon!"

He turned with an impatient scowl on his face that softened when he saw Ann. "Aye?"

"What news of Captain Carter?" Ann asked him, still scanning the harbor for his ship. The reek of fish and tar was overwhelming in the heat. The flies lit maddeningly on her hands and face.

Arch put down his buckets, spit on his palms, and rubbed them together. "We set sail on this tide," he said. He grinned, showing a gap where his front teeth had been kicked out. "Allender couldn't hold 'im."

"Thank God." Ann sighed with relief. "Thank you."

Arch looked over one shoulder and sidled closer to Ann. "They're saying John was shot."

"Yes."

"Smuggling, they say." Arch waited eagerly.

Ann took a step backward. "Smuggling? Who says it?"

"Tom Handy, for one," Arch replied. He winked broadly. "But I know it was an accident."

He hoisted his buckets and went on, leaving Ann in a cloud of tar fumes. She was glad to hear that Carter was freed and uncharged, worried to hear that Tom Handy spoke in the town of her brother's business. Smuggling was not a word she cared to hear connected so blithely and approvingly with John. Frowning, she turned into the traffic of barrows and wagons.

Roger was ahead of her.

Immediately Ann changed course, even though

she knew he had seen her, even though she had felt her heart leap and buck at the sight of him. She tried to cross the street, but a wagon trundled in front of her, barring her way. The sun was suddenly hotter and brighter, and she found it hard to breathe.

"Ann—Mistress MacKenzie?"

She hung her head and could think of nothing to say. She could not even raise her eyes to look at him. Her gaze took in the hem of her own plain dress and his dusty shoes as he stopped beside her. Ann could not forget that he had lied to her, had led her on in pleasant talk while hiding his identity. She had a sudden desire to slap him. She had a sudden desire to cry. She wished he were native born. She wished she could fly away.

"Why did you do it?" she said in a stifled voice.

"Do . . . ?"

Ann shook her head, shook away the question she wished to ask. She'd been caught off guard, but now she was strong. She challenged him, all her defenses now up. "Why did you shield my brother last night? It smacked of treason to me. As did your seditious talk on the beach."

Roger rubbed his chin and moved his shoulders uncomfortably under his faded jacket. "It was wrong of me not to tell you that I'm a sailor in His Majesty's Navy," he said. He turned and looked squarely at her. "And yet I did not feel like the king's man when we met."

A quick, fierce heat raced up Ann's back and neck and all the way through her at his words. The wagon moved on, and she began to walk blindly across the street, not knowing what to do or say or what to think. She understood his meaning but could not believe it.

"Last night—it was my apology to you," Roger explained, keeping step with her. "While I was in your house, I stood outside of my vow and loyalty."

"And now you are in it again?" Ann asked. She stopped in the shade of the same shed where Reliance had made her confidence. A trio of barefooted, wharf-haunting boys dodged past, hallooing and cat-calling. Warily Ann raised her eyes to Roger's face. "Are you the king's man today?"

Roger smiled. "Not when I am with you."

She caught her breath. Their eyes held for a long moment until Ann had to look away. A tremor went through her, a tremor which she wanted to believe was disgust. But there was a melting inside her that she fought hard against. She must resist it.

"A mate of yours is to be hanged," she said harshly.

"Ann—"

"He loved a Marblehead girl and would elope with her," she went on in a rush, hating herself for

113

speaking, hating him for being British. "The fool. The fish-headed fool."

Roger winced. "He lost his heart."

"He'll lose his life, now!"

Ann choked back a sob. All her known world had slipped awry, and she could not bring it back on course. "Why did you come here?" she whispered.

She put one hand against the shed to steady herself and saw two women of her mother's acquaintance pass by with curious looks. Her cheeks burned. "I must go."

"Wait—" Roger stood beside her in the shadow. He looked at her beseechingly. "I know I can only hurt you by speaking to you here in the town. But we had nothing between us on the beach. None overlooked us there."

Ann put her hands to her flaming cheeks, hardly knowing where she was. "I—I do sometimes walk up on Burial Hill to see the night fall," she stammered, and then blundered away from him through the crowd.

As she rounded a corner, Ann paused, closing her eyes and drawing a shaky breath. Had she lost her senses, she wondered, to have spoken so to a British sailor, to a man who might have shot her brother? She put an unsteady hand to a pile of lobster traps. She knew she could not return home yet, for her brother knew her too well and would notice her flushed cheeks and trembling voice. She wished she could loosen her bodice, for the air was stifling.

"Ann?"

She whirled around. Tom Handy stood watching her. Her pulse hammered dully.

"What—do you want?" she stammered.

Tom raised his eyebrows high, and he rubbed his nose in a gesture of exasperation. "Only to give you a good day."

"You needn't bother," Ann said. Her eyes narrowed. "You've been gossiping of my brother John, and I would have you leave off. He had his wound in an accident as the militia trained in the pasture."

Tom grinned. "Ah. So that's how it was."

"That's how it was," Ann insisted, beginning to move past him. "Now I'll give you a good day."

But Tom barred her way. "I saw that sailor speak to you just now. What did he want?"

"Only the offer of free beer," she lied. She lifted her chin and met his eyes squarely. "Now let me pass."

He held out both hands and stepped aside and watched her as she went. Ann walked slowly until reaching an alley, and then turned down it and fled.

Fool fool fool! Ann threw herself back against the wall of a house when she was safely alone and pressed the heels of her hands into her eyes until she saw stars. She didn't know what had possessed her to speak to Roger as she had, to make a tryst with him. This was not Ann MacKenzie. She was disjointed from herself and all that was familiar to her.

"I've lost my reason," she groaned, opening her eyes.

Ann watched a three-legged dog hop-step past her, its nose to the rocky ground and its glance sliding cautiously from side to side. It kept her warily in its sights, trusting nobody. More than anything, Ann wished she could confide in someone. She wanted to share her thoughts with a sympathetic heart, to puzzle out her motives and find a way out of what she'd done.

But John would sooner lock her in the cellar than discuss the feelings she had for a British sailor, and Judith's loyalty was wholly invested in John. And though her mother's heart had opened to her for a moment, she could not imagine ever confiding in Mistress MacKenzie. Before Ann's mind swam a vision of Reliance, pale, plain-faced, eyes brilliant with love. Then, as in a dream, Ann saw the vision hurled backward into darkness, Reliance's face distorted by grief.

Somewhere beyond a fence, a baby screamed and began to cry.

"Oh, God," Ann said, shaking away the dream in fright.

She had never heard of a more dreadful thing than what had befallen Reliance. This could not happen to her. This would not happen to her. She would not meet Roger that evening or any evening.

Squaring her shoulders, Ann hurried along the alley and made her way back to the Wild Rose. She paused when she reached Front Street, and rested her eyes on the bulk of the inn, serene and steady as a harbored ship in the sunlight. She saw her own window and the gray shingled roof, and the joints and corners where a hundred years of building had expanded it, and felt herself anchored again. She drew her breath and went in. In the tavern, her father was serving ale to several men.

"Ah, Ann, there you are," Mr. MacKenzie said warmly. "Where have you been?"

"I went to inquire after Captain Carter," Ann replied, thinking of her mother and unable to meet her father's eyes.

All the men nodded, their expressions grim. "He's unaccosted, by all accounts," said Mr. Devane. "Thank the good Lord."

"And no thanks to Allender," added a warehouse agent named Levi Crofut. He glared down his fleshy nose and gave his ale a dark look.

Ann put herself to work scrubbing the floor and let the old, reassuring conversation of the inn encircle her. This had been the thrust and import of all the talk she had ever heard in the tavern, the daily airing of grievances against the British. Taxes, tariffs, and duties, charters, deeds, and claims; absentee governors making foolhardy rules and settling suits with no regard to right or justice; monopolies granted indiscriminately to the English East India Company and prices bleeding the colonies dry; the infamy of Parliament, the carelessness of the king; the grumbling, rhetoric and a cautious call to arms —it was the litany and daily hymn of Massachusetts Bay, and it rekindled Ann's spirit to hear it. This was the Wild Rose Inn she had always loved, filled with familiar voices.

It brought her back to herself. As she scrubbed vigorously against the pitted floorboards on her hands and knees, she scoured away all softness, all vain and foolish imaginings. Her back ached, but she did not mind. It helped clear the clouds from her heart.

Behind her the conversation worked itself around to Reliance.

"The man is a black-souled bastard for seducing that girl," one man growled. "I'll hang him myself after Allender has done with him."

"There's one as deserves hanging," another joined in.

Ann's knuckles whitened as she gripped the boar-bristle brush.

"Reliance was always a foolish, headstrong girl," Crofut declared. "She had no sense nor caution in her."

"Braxton has beaten sense into her now,"

Devane said self-righteously. "She'll not quickly let another man beguile her, but will marry where she's told."

Ann clenched her teeth. Beguile? That was certainly what Roger had done, but why? And why such generosity from him, such mercy and care of her brother's life? It galled her to be beholden to him. Then, with cold certainty, Ann knew that he had done it for just that purpose, to put her into his debt. If his beguiling serpent's words were not sufficient, he would demand payment for his clemency. Ann scoured even harder. The rascal could wait until the sun came up, in that case, for she would not meet him anywhere on this earth.

"Oh!" she cried, dashing the brush into the bucket so hard that it splashed dirty water onto the wainscoting.

"Daughter!" Mr. MacKenzie called. "Have you hurt yourself?"

"No," Ann said through clenched teeth. "I have stopped myself in time."

Levi Crofut tapped his empty tankard and gave the other men a dour look. "Would that Reliance Braxton had been so careful."

"I do agree with you, Mr. Crofut," Ann said with passion. "Reliance was a fool, and the English are all dogs and scoundrels! I hate them!"

Her father came toward her, making quieting

motions with his hands. Ann scowled at him. "I won't be silent, I do hate them!"

"Ann, Ann!" He took her elbow and hauled her up none too gently and propelled her through the door. Ann went with him grudgingly, nursing her resentment. She didn't speak when her father led her outside and sat her down on an upturned bucket.

"Now, maid," Mr. MacKenzie began in a stern voice. "Temper yourself."

Ann folded her arms. She was close to tears, but she fought them back. "Why?" she asked. "Why, Father? Why are you so careful of giving offense to the British? Why do you serve them and make them welcome here?"

"We are *all* of us British," he said. "King George is yet our sovereign."

"And yet your own son lies wounded by the king's servants!" Ann grabbed her father's hands. "How can you be so meek and mild to them!"

Mr. MacKenzie looked suddenly tired. With a sigh, he settled himself on the ground with his back to the wall. He looked at Ann for a long while in silence, and then shook his head. He dug a little hole in the ground with one knotty forefinger.

"It is because John lies wounded that I act as I do," he said quietly. "I must temper his rash words and deeds with smooth ones. That is also why I have not tried to stop John's skylarking, for that is what

John must do. Otherwise he might turn to drink or violence or else ship out of Marblehead and we never to see him again in this world."

"Skylarking? Father, you call smuggling mere skylarking?" Ann demanded. Impatiently, she waved aside a horsefly.

He shrugged. "You see again how I soften everything that is hard and unlovely. It is what I must do, and what I do when Allender and his men are here."

"You could at least—"

"Do you think I like it?" he broke in. "It is wise to be meek and mild, for in this way I protect my own. I do not regret seeming overaccommodating, but do not think I like it."

Ann met her father's eyes, and a blush colored her cheeks. Indeed, he made no protest over the burden he made for himself to carry, had devoted his life to a woman he knew full well did not love him.

"No," she whispered. "I do not think you like it. I am sorry, Father."

"There, now." He patted her hand. "Let us not speak of sorry to one another, for we have nothing to forgive, you and I."

Ann held her father's hand to her cheek. She knew that if there was anyone in whom she could confide, it was her father, who was just and merciful. But she did not know how to talk of the thing that was most on her heart. It defied her power to speak.

"Father, do you think Reliance was a fool, and that her lover deserves hanging?" she asked.

"No one is made a fool by love," Mr. MacKenzie answered. "And no one deserves to die for it. Of that I am most solemnly sure."

"But in this case—"

"This case is a tragedy," her father went on. "Ann, do not judge those two young people harshly. You well know Reliance is a good girl. They were brave to take such a chance when so much was against them. That is a courage we must more of us have."

Ann nodded, her heart full. Her father had such courage, to accept the winks and nudges when Captain Carter was around, to smile at Captain Allender, to turn a blind eye when his son met ships in the dark, to make such hard choices to preserve his family and all he held dear. She hoped she would have such courage when it was needed.

Ann knew she must be brave enough to see what bargain Roger wished to make for John's safety. She would be on Burial Hill when dusk came.

Chapter Eight

THE LIGHT WAS beginning to change when Ann slipped out of the busy tavern and hurried upstairs. She smoothed her sleeves over her hard, slim arms, frowning over the task ahead. From a box by her bed, she took out a polished metal mirror. Ann fogged the surface with her breath and rubbed it to a sheen on her arm. Then she stood at the window, making a somber study of her reflection. Her blue eyes grew dark as she stared into them.

What did Roger see when he looked there? she mused. What did he look for and hope to find? Was he searching for the same things she was? Ann saw the color deepen in her cheeks at the thought of him, and she threw the mirror onto the bed.

Her appearance meant nothing. Roger meant nothing. He was a devil and a tyrant's tool, a lackey who deserved to be whipped for bargaining at a girl's virtue. She imagined how sweet would be her revenge if John died, how much she would enjoy denouncing Roger's treason to Allender.

"Oh, God," she whispered the next moment. "What am I thinking of?"

Ann paused on the threshold of her room, wondering if she should check on her brother. But she had seen the heady bright color in her own face, and he would, too. She hurried by the door of his chamber and stole down the back stairs.

The opposite door opened as Ann was hurrying across the parlor, and she jumped guiltily. Judith stopped in the doorway, as startled as she was.

"Oh, Ann," Judith said with a light laugh. "We are all on guard these days. We sneak about as though crossing enemy lines."

Ann's throat tightened. "Foolish, aren't we? Do you go to see John? I know he hopes you are coming."

"I brought him some blueberries," Judith said, lifting the splint basket that hung in the crook of her arm. "That should put the color in his cheeks."

Ann laughed a bit wildly. "They will if you smear them on his face."

Judith laughed, too. "If he makes trouble for me I vow I will apply them in that manner." She made for the stairs, but then stopped again. "Where are you going?"

"Only for a walk," Ann said. "You know 'tis my habit."

Judith frowned. "You're too solitary, I think. If only you had a sweetheart."

Ann silenced her by putting a hand over her mouth. She shook her head and smiled, feigning a lightness that she could not feel. "Do not worry for me," she said, plucking a blueberry from Judith's basket.

Then she turned and ran out of the room before her friend could say anything more. It went against her nature to lie to those she loved, and it pricked her resentment toward Roger yet more.

She hurried through the streets of Marblehead, her head back and her eyes bright with defiance. She could not wait to see Roger—to tell him how much she loathed him, how she had heard the truth and weighed his true worth through his honeyed words. How dare he dangle her brother's life over her? Ann lifted the hem of her dress, the faster to walk, as she rehearsed in her mind how she would repudiate him. She nearly ran up Burial Hill, whose top was still lit with the westering sun.

Breathless, Ann lunged up the path to the crest of the hill and stood there. Roger was nowhere in sight.

She turned this way and that, looking for him, trying to catch her breath, as a confusion of disappointment and anger settled onto her shoulders. After all that—and he was not there.

"Dog, the dog," she whispered. She tried to work up her anger and indignation again, and then gave it up.

Much deflated, she wiped her hand across her heated forehead and began to walk along the ridge of the hill among the headstones. From that distance, the ships that filled the harbor and beat their way out against the wind were small and toylike, and political wrangles were dwarfed by the ocean, which was deeper than hatred and stronger than men. The evening sun threw Ann's long shadow eastward, out to sea, as though pushing her, urging her gently, showing her the way. The tall grasses nodded their heavy heads as the breeze eased by and songbirds careened overhead and dipped down into the trees. Around her the markers read "Lost At Sea." The sea could swallow them, smooth the way over, and erase them all.

Ann sat with her back to a granite headstone still warm from the sun and hugged her arms around her knees. The breeze carried away the difficulties, the hardness, the enmity, and the fears. A stalk of grass waved beside her cheek, tapping her lightly. Ann sighed and put her head down on her folded arms. How sweet to find peace, how rare and good.

When she raised her head again, Roger was

climbing the hill toward her. She waited for the surge of anger and hate that should come. But it did not come.

Roger stooped to pluck up grasses, the golden sedge and the ruffed green timothy, the bluestem and silvery pearlgrass. On his face was the same grave, thoughtful pleasure that Ann had first seen, and she knew with a faraway hopeless certainty that she could not be angry with him, and could never hate him, come what may. She had felt a tie to him since they met, something that caused their eyes to meet across distances, something that caused her to hearken for his voice. There could be no hate when the sight of him made her want to run into his arms.

At last he stopped before her, and the setting sun struck gold into his hair. He smiled down at her. She did not rise.

"I didn't think you would come," he said.

His voice sent a shock of sweet hot confusion running through Ann. She hated to think he would blackmail her, but she could not look away from him.

"What do you want from me?" she asked, all defiance gone from her.

"What do I want?" he repeated with a frown. He had left his uniform jacket behind and stood there in shirt and breeches, stripped of his purpose and occupation.

"To keep silent about my brother," Ann whispered. "Why did you have to be this way?"

Roger knelt before her, still frowning. His blue-green eyes searched hers for understanding. "On my oath, I swear I don't know what you mean."

The neck of his shirt was open, and Ann could see the pulse beat strongly at the base of his throat. She wanted to put her finger there, wanted to press her hand to his chest to feel his English heart. She could not believe the thoughts that were in her. She knew she was lost. A tear rolled down her cheek.

"Ann, I don't ask anything for my silence," he said hoarsely. "I promise. Please don't cry."

"Then why do you do it?" she asked. "Why do you defy your captain?"

"Allender? I hate that man." Roger settled on the ground beside her and fingered the grasses he held in his hands. He began plaiting them as he spoke. "Allender's an Englishman and scorns all us Scots. He's also cruel and a coward. He's a man not worthy to be obeyed."

Ann felt herself suddenly prickle all over as though a new sense had been awakened. She stared at him, absently wiping her cheek. "You're a Scot?"

He grinned on one side of his mouth. "Aye, lass."

"But I didn't know." Ann caught her lower lip in her teeth. "Where—what part of Scotland is your home?"

"A wee scrap of a place called Kilbirnie," he said, his eyes looking out to sea. "Not far off the western coast. My family for many ages were yeomen, but the lands were used up and the family died out and I left a pauper. So I made my way to Glasgow, and that was where I took the king's shilling."

Ann was transfixed. "Glasgow—do you know a place called Arrochar at the end of the Firth of Clyde?"

"No." Roger looked down, braiding the grasses together into a hoop no broader than his hand. "Why does such a faraway place have meaning for an American girl?"

"That is where we MacKenzies hail from," Ann explained shyly. "I always wondered what it was like there. I—I had an ancestor named Bridget, and she left Arrochar when she was the age I am now. I feel a strong tie to her, though I never knew her."

"And what happened to your Bridie?" Roger asked.

"Ah, it is sad." Ann put her chin on her fists and shook her head slowly from side to side. She sighed, hearing soft birdsong.

"Sad how?"

"She fell in love with the wrong man," Ann said. "And she suffered for it."

Beside her Roger stirred and changed his position on the ground. He was frowning over his handiwork. "I don't believe you can fall in love with the wrong soul," he said quietly. "For if you love truly, how can it be wrong?"

Ann tilted her head to one side and looked away from him to hide the flush of color on her cheeks. She stared intently at a toppled gravemarker, memorizing the shallow carved lines of skull and bones. She knew it should make her think of mortality, but she could not think of such dark things. She thought instead of how rich and beautiful Roger's voice sounded in her ears and of how lovely it was to believe that what he said was true.

"Will you go back home when your service is over?" she asked, her voice muffled by her arm.

"Less and less I think I can," Roger said with a sigh. "There's nothing for me there any longer, and I must find a new place for myself. But it hurts me to say so, for 'tis very hard to give up your home."

"Tell me about Scotland," she begged.

"And what should I tell you?" Roger asked. "That she is hard and beautiful, and very fierce, and yet when you look at her you never wish for more nor—nor ever want to leave her—" His voice broke off.

Slowly Ann raised her head and found Roger gazing at her. The birdsong was stilled, and the breeze suspended. Ann felt the slow and giant revolution of the earth beneath her, and she could not look away.

"I—" she whispered. "I—"

A gull winged by just then, calling mournfully into the twilight. Ann looked away at last. Her pulse was racing.

"I must go."

Roger nodded and did not try to stop her. But he held out his woven band for her inspection. Each gold and green strand was deftly plaited into its neighbor, and the seed heads were arrayed around it like triumph-laurels. Ann touched it with one finger.

" 'Tis beautiful," she said.

Without speaking, Roger slipped it gently over her wrist and kept his hand on it. Ann looked down. Their hands, his worn by shipwork and hers worn by tavern work, twined fingers together, and the ring of grass slipped down around them like a wreath.

"Ann, darling Ann." His breath was warm on her neck. "This could be my home."

Ann leaned forward and rested her forehead against his shoulder, and felt his hand tighten over hers within the green-gold chain that bound them. She had never been so happy nor so filled with fear.

"This cannot be," she whispered. "There's nothing right in it."

"It is right. If you only will believe that, we can overcome," Roger said. "I am sure of it."

"I do wish I could believe that," Ann said. "Only I cannot." She pushed away from him and struggled to rise, and then ran, stumbling blindly down the hill.

Ann's sleep was troubled and filled with dreams that made her blush with shame when she awoke before dawn. She knelt by her window, waiting for the sun to come up over the harbor and thinking of Roger.

Being cast out of his home and only reluctantly in the King's Navy, he might have truly found some sympathy and accord in his heart for the colonists. Perhaps he honestly agreed with America's politics. Perhaps that was why he had scanted his duty to Allender. Perhaps the words he'd spoken at their first meeting were his true thoughts.

She propped her elbows on the sill and looked at the still-quiet forest of masts in the port. Perhaps Roger had already leaned in his heart toward America and now felt a stronger pull.

Perhaps, indeed, he loved her.

Ann drew her breath in sharply and looked out, filled with hope. He was out there, somewhere, perhaps thinking of her. The sun crested the horizon and shot directly into her eyes, dazzling her, throwing all its light onto her.

Then she shook her head. She could not fool herself that any man would desert for her, would risk all security for her. Will of God Handy would not give up his way of life for Bridie, and Roger would not risk hanging for Ann.

As the sun grew stronger, it cast her doubts into even starker relief. She hardly even knew Roger, did not even know his family name. It was the vainest conceit to imagine him deserting for her. She did not know him. She did not know him at all.

"But I do," she whispered, gripping the windowsill. "I have always known this man. Oh, God. What shall I do?"

To her surprise the windowsill shifted under the force of her hands. A board nailed beneath the sill had slipped down, and a crack was revealed. Ann sat back on her heels and carefully drew the board away. Behind it was a small bundle wrapped in a cloth.

Her heart pounded. With a gentle hand, Ann withdrew the package. The linen was yellowed and dry with age, and when she unfolded it, dust rose up and sailed softly in the morning sunlight. Folded in the cloth was a crude wooden doll and a blackened metal crucifix on a chain.

As Ann stared down at them, she felt the hair stir on the back of her neck. Bridie MacKenzie had hidden the things there. Of that she was certain.

"Oh, Bridie," Ann whispered. "Help me. Tell me what to do."

She waited. The only answer was the sun pouring more and more light into her room, filling it with radiance. The light touched the edge of the bed and slowly spread across it, then lit the candlestand with its pewter candlestick. At last the sunlight entirely covered the small table and illuminated the bracelet of grass that lay there.

Ann crossed the room and picked up the bracelet. She took a deep breath and closed her eyes. She almost expected to hear Bridie's voice, but only heard her own heart beating. This was what courage Reliance had felt, and Ann's whole being felt raised up above the world.

Then, while the room filled with light, Ann carefully replaced the doll and the cross in their cloth wrapping and stowed them reverently where she had found them. She laid the grass bracelet on them and pressed the board back into place to hide the silent treasure once again.

She knew she loved Roger. But she must hide that love safely away, or it would be destroyed as surely as dried grass thrown onto a flame.

Later in the morning, as she walked to the blacksmith with an iron pot for mending, she saw Judith coming toward her. Ann knew she would founder and be set adrift and keelless if she could not speak to even one person. Reliance would have understood, but Reliance was gone. Nor did Ann expect sympathy from her bitter mother. So she ran to meet Judith.

"Walk with me," she pleaded, taking her friend's elbow and turning her in the street. A woman opened a housedoor and tossed a bowlful of fish entrails into the dust.

"But I was on my way to John," Judith began, stepping daintily around the offal. She looked at Ann, and a worried frown creased her forehead. "Whatever is it, Ann? You look sick to death."

Ann nodded. "I need your counsel," she said, her voice trembling slightly. "You must hear me out and not speak until I have done."

Arm in arm, the girls walked up the street. For the first time in days, the sun hid behind clouds, but the air was as close as ever. Ahead, they heard the ringing of iron on iron, and together they entered the forge.

Trehearne, the deaf blacksmith, was blowing up the fire with his great bellows. It roared and pulsed like the heart of hell, throwing its lurid glow stroke upon stroke across the brawny man's face and leather-aproned frame. Trehearne was heating a horseshoe to the working stage as a massive gray gelding stood by, rolling its eyes whitely at the fire and shifting its feet. Ann put her hand to the beast's neck to gentle it. She had to look away from Judith as she spoke, or else she could not do it. She was not ashamed of loving Roger, but afraid to see how her friend would answer her.

"What's amiss?" Judith asked in a low, coaxing voice. "You must tell me."

Trehearne put the glowing shoe on the anvil, and brought the hammer down with a clang. A shower of sparks spewed forth, and Ann felt the blow in her bones.

"You wished me to have a sweetheart," Ann said.

"Yes?" Judith's voice rose with interest.

Ann smoothed the gray horse's neck, sensing fear and apprehension beneath her fingers. "You'll wish you'd never had such a thought, I think."

"Ann, you talk in riddles," Judith said, one eye on the sweating blacksmith. She placed one hand over Ann's and pulled her around to face her. Her gleaming hair burned copper-and-gold in the forge-light. "Do you love some man, now? Are you telling me you love some man your family would not welcome?"

A sob rose in Ann's throat, and the strident ring of hammer on anvil matched the painful beats of her heart. "Judith, I met a man and loved him at once. It was as you said it would be. I knew when it happened and could not mistake it for anything else. I love him so. But it was only after that I knew—that I saw—"

"Knew what? Saw what?"

Ann raised her eyes to Judith's, pleading for understanding. "He is one of Allender's men," she whispered.

Judith's face whitened. "Ann—no."

"It's true, Judith, and I cannot help myself!" Ann clutched her friend's hands. "You told me that country must not bar love, and it does not. But even so, he has no more love for England than do we!" she added in a rush.

Judith cast a terrified glance at Trehearne, although he could hear none of their words. He stoked the fire again, and the forge shimmered with heat. "But, Ann—" she faltered.

Ann tightened her grip on Judith's hands. "He saw John's wound and protected him from Allender's inquiring," she continued breathlessly. "His heart is with the Colonies. He does not love England. I believe he loves me."

Her voice died out to a whisper. Judith was silent as Trehearne fit the shoe to the gray's hoof, and the sharp smell of burnt horn filled the air. The horse struggled, hobbled by the blacksmith's grip. For all its size it was powerless.

"Ann, Ann," Judith said, her voice entreating. "What kind of wooing is this? He holds your brother's life in his hands. For this you love him?"

"No, not for it, but because he could but does not compel me," Ann breathed.

Judith put one hand to her cheek and shook

her head in dismay. "I don't know how you can admit such ideas into your head. Your brother is shot by one of Allender's men. How can you think of such a thing as loving a man who may have shot John?"

"I know, you cannot tell me anything I haven't thought of," Ann said. "But you bade me love where my heart told me I must. You *said* this to me! *He* is the man I love."

"Ann, you fool," Judith groaned. "Even if it is so, you've seen what disaster it is. Reliance is outcast, her hopes broken and her family suspect of English sympathies. Her lover will die, and his company will abuse us all the harder for it! This is all that you can look for in such a match."

"No."

"Yes, Ann. Yes. You cannot do this or you will wish you had never lived," Judith said. "Consider Reliance. Consider her lover. Consider these things before you wreck yourself."

Ann watched as Trehearne took the iron from the fire again, saw it gleam white hot in the dimness, watched the sparks struck from it on the anvil, the heat beating from it like a living heart. Then the blacksmith plunged the burning metal into a barrel of water, and the heat was extinguished with a great gasp of steam. When he drew it out again, the iron shoe was black and cold. Ann shuddered. To know

Roger was not in the world would be death to her now.

"Disaster," she said in a dull voice. "I won't see him again, Judith. I'll send him from me."

"Yes," her friend agreed with too much eagerness. "It is the only choice."

Ann nodded. She loved Roger. And she would give him up.

Chapter Nine

THE WILD ROSE INN seethed and churned with dire threats late that afternoon as fresh reports came in of the hardships and privations in Boston. The British blockade and closing of Boston Port was like a fist throttling the life out of that city. Folk were starving. There was no work. There were riots for bread. And the warships stood off the coast like carrion birds.

"It is a proper coward's act!" Penworthy exclaimed hotly. "To coerce a town by punishing its womenfolk and infants. The king would have us loyal subjects, but buys our loyalty with uncommon strange currency."

"Let them come at us who can fight," growled Jeremiah Bull, fingering a knife. "We will not be afraid to meet them."

There was rancorous approval for this, and another man slammed the table with the flat of his hand. "Let them tax us all they want," he said with a bloodthirsty scowl. "We'll pay with interest."

Ann stood by the kitchen door, hugging her arms around herself, listening to the surge and crash of protest that pounded like the surf against the walls of her house. On one side she heard "to the devil with the king and Parliament"; on another side she heard "smuggling is God's work in Massachusetts." Nat Trelawney lounged among a company of his mates, sipping his ale, grinning. His eyes swiveled around and met Ann's. He let out a silent laugh.

Ann felt again that uncanny, terrible feeling of strangeness in her own home. Here were the men she'd known all her life, in the house where she'd lived all her days, talking murder, tasting murder on their lips, swearing their most holy oaths on murder. And when they raised their flintlocks and boathooks and wolder sticks, they would not hesitate to sharpen their aim on Roger's back.

She pressed her temple with one hand and wondered if they could tell, these men, if they could see that her patriotism did not look and sound like theirs. Her allegiance was not her own any longer.

"Annie," came a quiet voice in her ear.

She whirled around, eyes wide. John was standing behind her in the doorway, grinning that he had made her jump.

"Quick as a cat tonight," he teased.

"We're all on the jump," she replied.

Ann hurried away from her brother and his knowing eyes, and heard the hail and chorus of welcome as he went into the tavern. He was more popular than ever, as word had slyly spread of his meeting with a British musketball. Ann went through the motions of her service, replenishing tankards, bringing fish stew and bread from the kitchen, and somehow finding words to respond to the constant gallantry and flirtation of the crowd. She felt numb and cast out from her own self. Never before had she felt so separate from her twin, never before had she felt their hearts so sundered, never had she felt such a stranger in her own home.

"Ann," said Penworthy as she set a tankard before him. "You look white as a clamshell."

"I—" She nodded, hearing John's voice raised behind her in the bars of the latest patriotic song. "I'll take some air," she murmured.

She was falling into two pieces. John's laugh rang out as she opened the street door and stood on the step. For a moment she honestly feared she was coming apart, and she grabbed the frame of the door to balance herself. From down the street she heard the tramp of feet and ribald laughter. A dozen of Allender's men turned the corner and came toward the Wild Rose, raising the dust as they went.

"Mistress Ann!" The beefy lieutenant made a low bow to her as he reached the inn. Ann pressed herself against the doorway. She saw Roger among the men, and her heart leaped.

Then she looked away. She must not look at him, though every cord and sinew in her seemed to push her toward him. It astonished her that all the world did not see how she loved him, that her heart was not plainly on her face.

"You'll find it crowded, sirs," Ann said tonelessly. "You might take better comfort at the ship."

"A crowd suits us very well, maid." The lieutenant put a hand on the doorframe by her shoulder, but she stepped aside.

With loud, self-conscious bantering, the British sailors, all but Roger, entered the Wild Rose. There was a sudden halt of the song and laughter within. Slowly Ann raised her eyes to Roger's face.

" 'Tis good to see you," he said.

"Please, do not speak to me," she whispered, forcing herself to look away.

He lifted one hand as though to touch her, and she drew back in alarm. Roger stiffened, but then nodded and went into the tavern. Her heart aching, Ann followed him.

The British men had claimed two tables and called for full rounds as Roger joined them. The Marblehead men were now hunched over their tankards, their voices low. The walls and windows of the tavern seemed to be watching.

"Ann," Mr. MacKenzie called to her.

She crossed to him and pitched her voice low. "Don't ask me to serve them," she begged.

"But, darling." Her father sent an anxious smile to the sailors as they called out for ale and began a risqué song. "I'll need your help. We both know John should keep his distance from them."

"And so should I," Ann whispered. She did not hear Roger's warm baritone among the others. "All the distance there is."

"What's that?" Mr. MacKenzie bent his head to hear her over the noise.

Shaking her head in resignation, Ann went to the press for tankards. She had vowed to give Roger up and put him from her mind, but that was impossible. He was there, and must be there, and she could not run away.

"Have you seen these local fishboys running through their militia drills?" a midshipman asked his mates loudly when the song was done. "I swear it was a right entertainment."

One of them guffawed. "Don't they know we're here for their protection?"

"Tell me," the lieutenant said, turning around and challenging the room. "What need have you for your own militias?"

"For the defense of our families against the savage Indians," John spoke up, his eyes glinting dangerously. "And you were glad enough of our militias' help against the Huron and the French during the wars for the Canadas."

"The French are gone," the lieutenant replied.

"But not the savages," John continued with exaggerated patience. "The wilderness is still full of Indians."

"Such as the ones that raided the ships in Boston and threw the tea into the harbor," Mr. Bull said slyly.

There were a few muffled laughs and nudging elbows among the Marblehead men. The wives of some of them had found traces of paint on the men's faces last Christmastime, found black horsehair wigs and feathers stuck into coat pockets. That nighttime raid had been conducted by strange Indians indeed, with blue eyes and green eyes, blond hair and red. But for all that, theirs had been a deadly purpose.

"Aye," spoke up Nat Trelawney. "That particular tribe is very bloody. Cutting throats is all their pleasure."

"You'd best be on your guard from them," Mr. Bull warned from his corner. "They're nettled something fierce and have no respect for the king's law. Take a good care of your backs, for they will soon break out."

Ann rattled two pewter mugs as she set them on the table. It was hard to breathe. She stopped in front of Roger. Their eyes met, and he moved as though to speak to her but she hurried away, blushing.

"We shall have war break out in our very house I fear," she said to her mother as she burst into the kitchen. "Why do men love so to bait one another? It's maddening!"

Mistress MacKenzie looked up from her accounts ledger with a wry grimace. Light from the western window threw her face into sharp relief. "You'll find many of them a disappointment, my girl. My advice is to keep well clear of them all." She went back to her books, her quill scratching briskly in the hot room.

Ann let out a dry, bitter laugh. "In this, Mother, I think we are now in full agreement." She threw back the plank trap in the floor and climbed into the cellar hole to draw a pitcher of ale from a cask. Above, her mother sat in her light, adding her columns of figures, making order where she could in an uncontrollable world.

When Ann returned to the crowded common room, she was met by an outburst from one table of young men. "Ann!" Tom Handy called out. "We've been debating."

"And when have you not been debating?" she

asked, trying to make her way to the English sailors with the pitcher. She had to squeeze by Handy and his fellows.

"With Reliance Braxton out of the town, we have fewer girls than ever," Tom went on. "And so we want to know which of us you'll choose?"

Ann stopped and turned on him with her most forbidding look. He grinned up at her from his chair and his gaze flicked just slightly toward Roger. His smile broadened.

Ann poured the jug full of ale into his lap. He gaped in astonishment and sprang up from his chair.

"I cry your pardon," Ann said coldly. "My hands were wet and the jug slipped."

Some of the others guffawed at Tom's discomfiture. He chuckled softly and sent Ann a look that made her rue her hasty temper.

"She's as sharp as ever her mother was," Mr. Bull chuckled. "And as pretty."

"Can you not choose among the local men?" Tom went on in a quiet voice. "Or do you have a taste for imported stock? Does the habit of bringing in outside refreshment run in this family?"

Ann went pale.

"Steady, steady, Tom," counseled Mr. Devane from the next table. He frowned and shook his head, glancing once at the British sailors in warning.

"No," Tom said, louder and angrier now. "I say

let Ann tell us. Will she prove herself as Reliance Braxton did, or will she assure that she is a true Patriot by choosing among us?"

"Don't rush her choice," the lieutenant taunted, standing up and sauntering toward Ann. He eyed her frankly up and down. "Let her try an English-man first."

The room fell silent. A chair clattered to the floor as Roger abruptly rose. "Sir—" His face was white.

"What?" The lieutenant grinned. "Did you hope to get at her yourself? You may, but you'll have to wait your turn."

"Bastard!" John roared out, and at the same moment, Roger threw himself across the table at the lieutenant and hurled him to the floor.

In seconds nearly the entire company of men was engaged in the fray. Ann shrank back against a table, staring as the men brawled wildly. She could not believe it had flared up so fast. Her father and other levelheaded souls hauled out first one and then another man by the back of the collar, urging calm and rationality, but each one plucked out of the fight threw himself back in with shouts of vengeance. Benches and tables were overturned, and heads were broken. Ann ducked as a pewter tankard flew past her head. She was disgusted and dismayed. She knew she should be glad that Roger had defied his superior for her sake, and that all the men of the town were ready to defend her. But she was not glad. She only knew the men were readying for war and would seize upon any provocation to join battle.

Across the room she met her mother's eyes. Mistress MacKenzie stood in the doorway, looking at her with a dark, impenetrable gaze. Then, shaking her head, she went away again.

As two men with bloodied noses wrestled at Ann's feet, she picked up her hem. She watched Roger take a fist in the gut and felt sick and angry and humiliated. She couldn't bear to watch anymore, and with a burning face Ann left by the front door.

"And they may all kill one another for all I care," she cried, wiping the tears from her eyes.

The fight was not without its casualties. When Ann returned home later, just after sunset, she found her brother nursing his wounded shoulder in the kitchen and her mother washing a bloody cut on Nat's forehead.

"You idiots," Ann said, wearily sitting down at the table. "What do you care what that pig says of me?"

John splashed ale into a cup and drank it down slowly, watching her over the rim. Fresh blood had seeped from his wound through his shirt, and his face was drawn. "I care more that the other one cares, Ann," he said finally.

"Aye," joined Nat. He sucked his teeth.

"I don't know what you mean," Ann muttered, resting her elbows on the table. "It was a stupid excuse for braining one another."

Mistress MacKenzie wrung out a bloodied cloth in a basin of water. "And for getting your father taken in."

Ann stiffened. "What do you mean?"

"She means our father as host and proprietor of this place, along with some others, is in custody," John said, leaning toward her with a scowl that distorted his handsome face. "And it is from a fight that none of *us* began."

Ann felt paralyzed. Part of her heart went out to her poor father, but the largest part of her care was there, in that room, facing a fierce brother she did not know. He continued watching her.

"Who is he?" he said at last. "He was here when I had my wound. You two had some exchange, then. What are his designs?"

"He has none that I know of." Ann licked her lips. She saw her hands tremble, and she sat on them to keep them still. "Perhaps he is a gentleman."

John suddenly dashed his cup off the table, and its contents splashed into the fire with a hiss. Ann drew back, her heart racing.

"Do not speak to me of gentlemen," John shouted, standing up and leaning across the table on both hands. "This is no place to speak of gentlemen. This is *not* England. Hear me, Ann. The King's Navy is here for one purpose, and that is to thwart and constrain us. If Allender and his men choose to do so by deceiving foolish girls like you, it only proves that they are despicable and deserve nothing less than hanging."

"They are not all like Allender," Ann whispered. "They are not all bad."

"And how would you know that?" Mistress MacKenzie asked as she wrung out the bloody cloth in the basin of water.

Ann swallowed the hard lump in her throat. John came around the table and gripped her shoulder hard. "Ann, if I thought you had any friendship for an Englishman—"

"You're hurting me!" Ann jerked away from him, her own temper flaring. "Don't threaten me, John! You do not master me!"

They glared at one another for a long moment, until John relaxed into a quicksilver smile.

"Ann, Ann, what are we doing?" he laughed, bending down to retrieve his cup. He poured more ale and gulped half of it down. "You see how they set us against ourselves."

Ann still sat rigid. "Would you beat me, John?" she asked in a quiet voice. "Would you kill me?"

"Don't carry on so," he said. He sipped his ale. "We're one, Ann, you and I. We are of one heart and one mind, as we ever were. Here, my girl."

He held his cup to her and in spite of herself, she took it and brought it slowly to her lips. The scent of ale that had always meant home to her now rose bitterly in her face. There was no communion any longer.

"I'm going out," she said, setting the cup down untasted.

"Ann—"

Ignoring her brother, Ann went through the door and let herself out of the garden and walked down the street. Above her bats jigged and skittered, black against a sky that still gleamed pale gray and pink. Faint candlelight came from windows, and voices, and the smell of food and smoke. Without conscious thought Ann took the path that led up Burial Hill. She was drawn to it and could go to no other place. She climbed slowly, touching gravestones as she passed them. Lost at sea, they read in letters dissolving in the dusk.

Near the top of the hill, Ann lifted her gaze and saw Roger waiting for her.

"Oh." Ann sighed, and he ran the last few yards that separated them. Ann stepped into his embrace and began to cry against him. "What have we done?"

"I'm sorry," Roger said, his cheek on her hair.

His arms were tight around her, and his heart beat against hers.

"I want to hate you."

"There can never be hate between us," he whispered. "You know that."

Ann pulled away from him. There was a cut on his cheek, and she touched it with trembling fingers. "You will kill my brother, or he will kill you," she said brokenly. "Whatever happens will break my heart."

"Ann, I don't wish to hurt you, nor your brother," Roger said, looking at her and smoothing her hair. He took her hand from his cheek and kissed her palm. Ann's heart ached. "But I do love you and I think you love me," he whispered against her hand. "I knew it from the start, as did you."

"No," she murmured, closing her eyes, feeling his lips caress the inside of her wrist. "I do not love you."

But she put her arms around him, and his encircled her, and she knew he understood. She sighed, resting her cheek against his shoulder. She could no more give him up than she could stop her heart from beating. That certainty was as strong as his embrace.

Then something made her look around. Nat was walking up the hill toward them. He stopped, their eyes met, and Ann felt the ground drop away beneath her. Very slowly Nat turned around and disappeared down the path the way he had come.

Ann tried to speak, to call out, but her voice caught in her throat.

"Who was that?" Roger asked.

"My brother's friend, and a devil," Ann whispered, breaking away from him. Her legs began to shake.

"Ann, you've done nothing wrong," Roger insisted.

Ann looked at Roger bleakly and shook her head. "I have done everything wrong," she said in a daze. "And yet there is nothing I can do now which would not be wrong." She began to hurry down the hill.

"Ann, please wait."

She stopped, her breath catching in her throat. But she could not turn back to him. Time was flying before her down the path.

If she reached John before Nat did, she could speak to him, make him understand. But she knew she had already lost. Closing her ears to Roger's call, she raced on down the hill and through town, past the lighted windows and barking dogs to confront her brother. Ahead she saw the roof of the Wild Rose above other roofs. With growing panic, she turned the corner. John was coming through the gate.

"Ann MacKenzie!" he yelled.

She stopped, and her brother strode toward her and grabbed her hand.

"Let me go!" Ann cried as he began to drag her back to the inn. She scratched at his hand, but his grip was like iron. She stumbled after him, bracing herself for what would come.

He wrenched open the house door and flung her inside. Ann caught herself against the kitchen table and whirled around to face him.

"Tell me Nat is a liar," John said, breathing hard.

Ann stared at him silently.

"I give you this chance to tell me Nat is a liar," John said again.

Still Ann said nothing. From the corner of her eye she saw Nat himself sitting in a corner, cleaning his fingernails with a knife, watching them. She wished him in hell.

John took a step toward her and raised one hand. Ann lifted her chin. "You are stronger than I am, John," she said. "But if you hit me, you are no brother of mine."

Slowly John lowered his hand to her cheek, and pressed it against her. He trembled, and his eyes were wide and shot with blood as he gripped her jaw.

"If I see that man in your company again," he said in a low voice, "I will kill him."

"You wouldn't dare to do it."

He smiled, then, a hard and joyless smile. "I would dare, Ann. I swear to you I would. And perhaps I will not wait until he molests you again. When next I meet him, we'll have a reckoning."

Chapter Ten

THE NEXT MORNING brought the first rain in weeks. Ann awoke to the sound of it pattering on white windowpanes and on the roof above her head. For a moment she lay in the vague, underwater light like one adrift. Then the tide of terrible facts came rushing back to her. She dressed quickly and threw a shawl around her shoulders.

She paused, listening, in the upstairs hallway. There were a few paying lodgers, but there was no sound from those quarters. The inn was silent but for the soft sighs and settling sounds that it always made. Ann tiptoed down the stairs and opened the door. A wet and bedraggled cat bolted in as she let herself out.

Ann covered her head with the shawl and clutched it tight under her chin. She must find Roger, must see him once more to warn him. But she was wary of everyone, of Tom Handy, of Nat Trelawney, of anyone in Marblehead who felt it his right to watch Ann MacKenzie. She kept close under the shelter of houses as she hurried down the street. The town was shrouded in mist from the harbor and the ocean beyond. Water dripped steadily all around and collected in pools. Drops of mist clung to Ann's eyelashes and to broken spiderwebs, and mud caked heavily underfoot. All sound was muted and strained, but sudden noises started out of the silence: a lowing cow; the creak of a rocking ship in the harbor; one lone kittiwake crying overhead. Ann was cold.

She went to the house of Judith's mistress, and scratched on the back door. Judith opened it a crack with a look of surprise when she saw Ann.

"Whatever is it?" she asked, looking past Ann's shoulder. She put out her hand. "Come into the house out of the wet."

Ann shook her head. "Help me. Judith, you must help me. It's John."

"What has happened?" Judith's eyes went black with fear. "Is he hurt? Is he dead?"

"No, but he's heading for the gallows, I swear," Ann whispered. "He is sworn to kill Roger whenever and wherever he meets him. You must take a message from me to Roger and warn him, for I dare not do it myself."

Judith drew her breath in with a hiss. "Nay, Ann! I will not."

Ann was chilled to the bone with the damp. Her skin felt like the skin of a drowned woman. "Judith, if my brother attacks and kills one of the King's Navy, he'll hang for it," she said, shivering.

"Oh, Ann." Judith put her face in her hands. "What have you done?"

"Only what you have done," Ann replied urgently. "I would not let the man I love be killed, nor will you. We did not choose where to love, and now we may not choose to give them up for lost."

Judith took an oilskin cape from a peg inside the door and drew it around her. "Let us hurry, then."

Her face was set and grim, but she linked her arm through Ann's. Side by side they hurried through the town to the harbor. Allender's *Southampton* lay at anchor, and through the fog they could dimly see men stirring on her.

"He may be on the ship," Judith said, hunching her shoulders within her cape. "I will not go out there."

Ann was scanning the seaport, looking among the men who were already about. All was vague and shadowy and gray, but then, through the mist, she caught a glimpse of a blond head. She clutched Judith's elbow. "He is there," she whispered, aching at the sight of him. He was with three companions, walking toward where Ann and Judith stood.

Before Roger could see her, Ann ducked behind a stack of casks. She watched Judith, who stood irresolute, rain slanting onto her cheeks. Ann heard the English voices come nearer, and she saw Judith stiffen and withdraw into her cape.

"I would speak to you," Judith said.

Spying between the barrels, Ann saw the four sailors stop. The fog wreathed around them like smoke. Roger's companions surrounded Judith, and one of them tipped back her hood.

"What hair," he said. "Who needs the sun when you can look on that?"

Judith stepped backward. "Don't touch me," she spat.

Ann bowed her head.

"You, sir," Judith said. "Can we speak privately?"

Hoots and laughter greeted this remark, but Roger's voice cut through them. "I'll be with you in a moment," he said to his mates. "I'll see what this maid wants."

Judith moved away, and Roger followed her.

"I carry a message for you," Judith murmured. "And though I love Ann, I don't do it for her sake or yours, but for her brother's."

"What is it?"

Ann listened to Roger's voice and was so filled

with regret that she couldn't even cry. The rain dripped steadily down, hissing into the water. She felt low and vile, skulking in the rain, eavesdropping, forcing her friend into the eye of the lewd sailors. But she loved Roger too much to do otherwise. She knew what Reliance had known: that she would give up her friends for the man she loved.

"Ann's brother has sworn to kill you," Judith said. "You'd best keep to your ship if you can."

"I cannot do that."

"Then steer clear of the Wild Rose and beware of John MacKenzie," Judith said harshly. "He's a fool for vengeance, and Ann is his other self. He'd sooner die than see her pledged to you."

"Where is she? Why could she not come herself? Does he keep her away?" Roger's voice was low and urgent.

"That does not—"

"Where *is* she?"

At that point Ann could no longer bear the fact that she was hiding, cringing behind barrels like a criminal on the run. She stepped out.

Judith looked stricken. "No," she cried out, shaking her head. "Don't, Ann."

Ann dragged her eyes away from Roger. "Please watch out for John for me," she begged her friend. Roger came to her, and they stood in the lee of the barrels. He tried to take her hand, but she would not let him.

"Ann, come away with me," he said hoarsely.

"Run away in the night, as Reliance did?" Ann wiped the rain from her cheeks. "I will not. I can not."

"Why?"

Ann searched his eyes for understanding. "Don't you see that this is impossible?" she asked. "Everyone is in league against this."

"That does not mean it is wrong," Roger said. "Ann, don't give your brother the ruling of your heart. If we love one another there can be no wrong."

"No, but to run away like thieves would be to say so. And I fear it does mean one of us is likely to die for it."

"You are still swayed by your brother's opinion," Roger said. "Ann, think for yourself, think of us."

Ann felt her throat tighten with the fear that gripped her. "I do think for myself, now. I am not a child any longer, and so I do think of you and of how hard and deadly this world truly is, no matter what I wish otherwise."

Roger took her by the arms as water dripped from his hair and onto his cheeks, shining like tears on his lashes. "Hard and deadly, yes. So do not turn us both into it alone. We must face it together. Trust what you feel," he pleaded. "That is faith."

"What I feel is disaster," Ann said, her whole

162

body shaking. "For the sake of preserving your life I cannot see you again. Don't make me ask you to desert for me. I won't be the cause of your hanging."

He frowned. "Ann, don't be afraid, only—"

Then John's sharp voice came to them. "Judith, where is my sister?"

Ann pushed at Roger with both hands. "Slip away. Run," she whispered.

But Roger did not move. John appeared in the opening of their shelter, his wounded arm in a sling. "Get out here," he said, his voice coldly calm. "Get out here so I can whip you back to hell where you belong."

"I won't fight you," Roger said.

"You coward," John shouted as he lunged forward and grabbed the front of Roger's shirt. Ann screamed and tried to force herself between them, but her brother threw himself backward, pulling Roger with him. They tumbled out onto the wharf, and then scrambled to regain their feet as the gulls and kittiwakes flew up with startled cries. John and Roger stood panting, watching one another, and a crowd of 'Headers quickly formed around them.

"Throw him in the drink, MacKenzie!" called one man.

"I won't fight you," Roger repeated, raising his voice as his English companions ran up. "I won't fight an injured man."

John yanked the sling from around his neck and threw it in the mud.

"Then my injury is no more," he said, and then bent down and hurled himself at Roger's legs. They went sprawling again. Ann cried out and tried to run toward them, but someone caught her arms behind her back and kept her away. She watched in silence as John began to pummel Roger with his good arm.

"Fight back, Rog!" one of the British sailors yelled. "Get him where it hurts!"

Roger threw himself to one side, rolled away and jumped up as quick as a cat. There was a bleeding cut on his lip, and he was smeared with mud. John struggled awkwardly to his knees, his eyes narrow with hatred. Blood showed at his shoulder and spread pinkly through his wet shirt.

"Fight!" the crowd yelled. "Don't just dance with each other."

Roger wiped his mouth with the back of his hand. "I wouldn't fight this boy," he said disdainfully. "Send him back to the schoolmaster." He deliberately turned his back on John and began to walk away.

"No!" Ann screamed as her brother leaped up and dove for Roger with his fist hard in his back. Roger stumbled and fell at the feet of a local man who grinned as he kicked Roger in the chin. Ann turned quickly away, her eyes shut tight as the other

English sailors helped Roger to his feet. Rain streamed down her face with her tears.

"Now it's beginning to look like a decent cock-fight," a man from the ropewalks laughed. "Have at him, John. We'll get the tar and feathers."

"Clip his other wing," a midshipman said, shoving Roger back toward John, who still struggled for breath in the mud.

Roger walked unsteadily, his back twisted with pain, and two of his companions grabbed his arms roughly.

"Get him out of here," Judith said in a shaking voice. "Take him away."

Judith bent to help John, who was struggling to rise with one hand pressed against his wounded shoulder. Ann felt as though she were tied in place with thick cables, for she could neither follow Roger nor help her brother. She thought she was going to be sick. As Roger was dragged away, he looked back with a dark look at John. Ann shuddered at what he must be thinking.

The crowd scattered, disgusted at losing a fine spectacle on such a drab day. The seabirds settled down on the pilings again and hunched their shoulders.

"Ann," John said with a gasp. He breathed hard through his nose, his nostrils pinched with pain as Judith supported him to his feet. "Come home."

Ann looked at him stonily. "You can no more

compel my loyalty through force than the king can yours," she said, looking into the blue eyes that had once been mirrors of her own. "You have taught me to love rebellion, Brother. You must not wonder at what may happen now."

He stared back, dismay spreading through his face. "Ann," he whispered again. "Don't do this. We are family."

Shaking her head, Ann turned and walked home through the pitiless rain, crying with an aching, depthless sorrow. All was lost.

The day remained gray and grim, and when the night fell it was as though the sun had given up hope and retreated forever. Darkness closed in with the fog. The night was cool for late August, and the air drew mist off the warm water. The fog slouched along the streets and footpaths of Marblehead, nosing among damp disgruntled chickens and making the minister turn up his black collar as he hurried to the home of a dying woman. The fog stole up the walls and pressed itself against windowpanes to frighten babies in their sleep and crept into stables where the horses swiveled their eyes and stamped. In the harbor, boats became ghosts of themselves, and fishermen going out on the tide yearned for their hearths and their pipes and cast their eyes more astern than to the sea.

At the Wild Rose Inn the front room was quiet. Mr. MacKenzie, released during the day from Allender's custody, sat brooding by a smoky fire, and his patrons sat in morose, respectful silence, glancing at him from time to time and shaking their heads over their tankards.

"It is a bad bad thing," Mr. Penworthy muttered to no one in particular. He scratched his head, pushing his old wig awry. "This is surely a bad time we are in."

"A bad and bloody time," added Mr. Devane.

Ann leaned against the wall, her hands clenched in her apron. She felt as heavy and silent as one of the stones on Burial Hill, and it seemed almost that the fog had invaded her body and her heart, and that she was lost inside her own self.

It was terrible to her that she was separated from her brother so entirely. She rued his violent temper and her own quick angers. There must be some reconciliation, she told herself dully. But she doubted that such a thing could happen any more than the colonies could embrace the Crown once more. And Roger—she could not bear to think of Roger.

Her father, rousing himself from his reverie, looked around and motioned to Ann to bring the men some more ale. She pushed herself wearily away from the wall and went through to the kitchen. There had been little mention of that morning's fight between John and Roger. Mistress MacKenzie had said simply that John did not need to be further provoked in his current state. And Mr. MacKenzie reminded Ann to think of the good of the family. Ann had said nothing. Her mother, as always, was tending the food as it cooked.

"Is John in the house?" she asked as she filled a jug from a barrel.

Mistress MacKenzie glanced at her from under her black brows. She turned back to the fire and flicked a drop of water onto a pan to test its heat.

"Nat Trelawney came around for him."

Ann set the full jug down heavily, and ale slopped over the rim. She swallowed hard, and looked at her mother. "Why won't you stop him?"

"Do you think I could?" Mistress MacKenzie retorted, her voice brittle and bitter as it so often was. "Do you think any woman can stop any man from throwing himself at death?"

The image of John's face danced before Ann's eyes, and then it dissolved and became Roger's— Roger's face smiling and grave and thoughtful. She squeezed her hands together.

"Yes," she said faintly. "Yes, if you have the faith to do it."

"Faith?" Mistress MacKenzie let out a shaking breath. "Have *you* such faith, Ann?"

Ann met her mother's challenging eyes for a

moment, but then she had to look away. "I don't know," she whispered brokenly. "I don't know."

As they stood there, facing one another across the scarred table, the back door opened and Roger stepped into the light, instantly meeting Ann's eyes. She swayed and gripped the back of a chair.

"What brings you here?" she choked out.

"Your brother," Roger answered. "Where is he?"

Ann's throat closed tight. She stared at him, wanting only to go to him; but she felt her mother's eyes on her and she dared not move. He came close to her and shook her arm. "Tell him he must not go out this night," he said in a low, intense voice.

"Why?" Ann choked. Her mother was staring at her.

"Allender is sworn to capture John MacKenzie and Nat Trelawney, for he has testimony to their actions."

Ann's mind reeled. "Testimony? Where from? *Who* told him this?"

"Handy," Roger said curtly. "Now tell me, has John left the house?"

"He—he is not here," Ann said in confusion. She tried to steady herself and gather her thoughts. She could not forget the look that Roger had given to John that morning, and his mere presence beside her sent her heart and her mind into wild confusion. She searched his face desperately, pleadingly, trying to blot out the clamoring fear in her heart.

"Tell me where he is, then, for Allender will catch him in the act," Roger said quickly, glancing toward the kitchen door. "Tell me, and I may warn him away."

"He is—" Ann saw her mother again, saw her hard, unyielding, skeptical eyes, and was overwhelmed by doubt. Roger had no cause to wish John well. Cold misgiving twined itself around her like the fog. *A trap, a trap, and a rope for John's neck.*

"Ann," Roger whispered. His eyes pleaded with her. "You must decide to trust me. Have faith in me."

She moaned. "Oh, dear God."

There was a commotion in the front of the house, and Mistress MacKenzie made a cutting motion with her hand. "Say nothing," she warned.

Even as she spoke, the door burst open, and Allender strode into the room.

Chapter Eleven

ROGER DREW HIMSELF up sharply and saluted. "No sign of him, sir," he said, his eyes straight ahead.

Ann took two steps backward and knocked over an empty bucket. As it went trundling loudly across the floor, she sent one frightened look at Allender, and then stared at her feet. Her father appeared in the door behind the captain, his usually gentle eyes hard and watchful.

"Where is your son, madam?" Captain Allender said as he walked around Mistress MacKenzie in a slow circle.

"I have told you he is not here," Mr. MacKenzie spoke up. He came into the room and stood by his wife's side with one arm around her. "Do not attempt to frighten Mistress MacKenzie, for I warn you, she is fearless and will not break. You'll only show yourself the bully you are if you bluster and rail at her."

Captain Allender's face flushed wrathfully dark. "You MacKenzies are a pack of rogues, every one of you," he fumed, glaring at Ann's father. "And you're the worst of all with your mild ways and your hostly smiles. You've been shielding a nest of serpents here."

Allender stepped forward abruptly and struck Mr. MacKenzie across the face so hard that Ann's father was thrown to his knees in the hearth, and his hands went into the hot coals. He yanked them out with a stifled oath.

A potent silence gripped the kitchen. Ann stared in horror at her father. Mistress MacKenzie knelt by him, drew close a bucket of water, and put his hands in it. Their profiles were charged with firelight. Across the room, Roger stood rigid, his face pale. The line of his jaw shifted as he clenched his teeth. Allender raised his chin and looked down at Ann's parents. He, too, was pale with fury and frustration.

Mr. MacKenzie broke the silence, his head lowered over his burned hands. "I have told you my son is not here," he said quietly. "And now I'll ask you to leave my house."

Allender barked at Roger to follow him and left the kitchen in a seething rage. Ann dared not look at Roger as he passed her.

"Post a guard!" the captain shouted to the rest of the regiment in the tavern. "When John MacKenzie comes home, arrest him. Watch MacKenzie and his wife."

Ann and her parents stayed in the kitchen, motionless and silent. They heard the tramping of the company leave the Wild Rose, and then it was unnaturally quiet. Not one man in the front room was speaking. Ann could almost see through the walls— see the watchful, vengeful eyes locked on the guard. The Wild Rose Inn, heavy and dull with the damp sea air, seemed to swell with slow waking as the lingering waves of Allender's violence eddied through the doors and hallways.

"Ann," Mr. MacKenzie said in a low voice. "Find your brother."

She was pressed against the wall and could only stare at him unblinking.

"Ann, they'll be putting out in longboats," her father continued, looking at her steadily. "They'll not rely on the *Southampton* but will lie for John in the coves and inlets. They'll take him when he's laden down with contraband and cannot maneuver, and they'll shoot him or hang him."

"They all believe you are a weak and harmless girl," her mother said. "Are you?"

"Find your *brother,* Ann," Mr. MacKenzie repeated with low urgency. "Go."

Without a word, Ann fled through the door

into the dark garden. The mist had hardened to rain again, and Ann was soaked to the skin as she fumbled the catch of the garden gate, feeling the ghostly touch of wet roses nodding against her cheek. Then she was out in the empty street, running in the rain.

Ann knew that if John and Nat followed their common course, they would be lying off the end of the Neck, hard by Lasque's Ledge. But it would take a precious long time to run all the way out there, and her clothes were already heavy with rain. She paused, thinking, thinking of Allender's boats.

There was no choice. Ann caught up her dress in both hands and raced for the water. The rain mumbled in her ears and dragged at her hair and at her hem. She stumbled and clambered down among rocks. A swift glance at the port showed her the dark and silent shape of a schooner—*Southampton*. It would soon move into the current, and its boats would lower. Fighting back panic, she reached down, waving her hands back and forth in the darkness among the wet rocks.

Her heart lurched as she touched a cold, weed-slimed painter. She hauled on it, drawing the dark shape of a boat toward her. Her hands fumbled under the gunwales for oars. There were none. Fighting panic, she crept along the slippery rocks to find another painter, another small craft. She hauled one toward her, and her hands met a pair of oars carelessly left on board. Clumsily she stepped in, and then slipped the painter from the iron ring embedded in the rock. Instantly the wooden craft knocked and ground against the rocks, pushed by the swells. Ann groped for the oars and wrestled them into the oarlocks. Her clothes clung to her, and her hair hung on her cheeks like seaweed. She looked over her shoulder, trying to steady her harsh breathing and make out the shape of the Neck across the water. The rain was letting up.

As she strained to see, the darkness resolved into shades of black and deeper black. Her destination lay across the harbor, across the line of the outrushing tide. She put her back to it and hauled on the oars.

In a moment she felt the grip of the current beneath her. She must bear as straight as she could across it, for it would carry her out fearfully fast. If she did not reach the Neck before the tide carried her past it, she'd be out to sea in the black night. Ann rowed, her hands rubbing against the wet oars, the tide taking her, taking her.

"No, I won't be taken where I won't go," she said through gritted teeth. "I won't." Above her the clouds began to break apart, and a wan light showed among the cracks. The rain was dissolving into mist again, writhing above the water.

And then she was in the spate, the current swift and strong and heedless. There was a cool wind out in the throat of the harbor, but Ann's back was on fire as she fought against the water. Her palms stung savagely with each pull on the oars. She looked over her shoulder and saw the black hump of the Neck rising against the sky and slipping past.

"Keep your light shuttered, John," she prayed. "Show no light."

Then, across the splash of her oars and the ragged sound of her own breathing, Ann heard another sound, the sound of several pairs of oars following not too distantly in her wake.

"Sink, you murderers," she gasped, pulling even harder and looking over her shoulder. Very near was the end of the Neck silhouetted faintly against the night. She was very near being taken out. "No!"

There was no thought in her but to beat the tide and save her brother. There was only Ann and the boat, and the water.

As she strained at the oars, she felt her boat fight its way out of the strongest current, and she hauled toward the rocks. The sound of following boats was louder, and now as the sky was opening the moon shone fitfully on the water and the wind grew stronger. Three boats, with three pairs of oars apiece, were swiftly closing the distance. Behind her, the water sucked and surged against the jagged rocks, foaming whitely.

Ann raised her oars, fearful to make the slightest sound. She hoped the British were not yet familiar with these waters as she was. They must go more carefully, feeling their way among the rocks. She felt her boat riding the current out, hurried by the wind.

Then she saw a light ahead.

"No!" Ann screamed.

The British boats had seen the light, too, for they changed course to make for it. Ann threw herself to her oars, using the tide and the current both to take her to her brother. His lantern was unshuttered again and answered from out at sea.

"John, no!" Ann screamed.

"Get him!" came a shout from the British boats.

Simultaneously Ann's boat and one of theirs slipped out from the shelter of the Neck and were buffeted by the wind of the Atlantic. Overhead, the clouds were racing across the face of the moon, and by its light Ann saw John and Nat just ahead, their boat tethered to a rock at the very end of the Neck. The British boat was headed straight for it, and Ann knew they meant to ram it. Nat knew it, too, for he was frantically grappling to untie the painter. The water boiled against the rocks, white on black. Ann saw Allender stand in the bow of his boat. He steadied himself, a pistol in one hand.

With a great heave, Ann dug one oar into the water and plowed her boat toward Allender's. But as Allender raised his arm to take aim at her brother, Roger lunged upward, and dove for John. The British boat collided with the smugglers', and John and

Roger toppled overboard. A shot exploded and they disappeared as a cloud streaked over the moon to bring down the darkness.

"NO!" Ann screamed.

She leaned on the gunwales, feeling the breath of the ocean fume upward to her face. Angry shouts came from the British boats, and Nat's dinghy cracked hollowly against the rocks. Ann plunged her oars into the water to keep from drifting and looked frantically around at the tossing waves. There was a howling empty sound inside her, and she could scarcely breathe. Her heart had fallen overboard and had plummeted into the black ocean. There was no sign of Roger.

Then, there was a splash and a gulping gasp for air beside her boat. One oar bucked in her hand as someone grabbed it.

"Annie," John choked. He threw one arm over the gunwales, and then one leg. Ann grabbed his wet clothing and dragged at him, hauling him in. John fell into the bottom of the boat, water streaming from him.

"Row," he gasped. "Get us around the Neck to Swampscott."

"Where's Roger?" Ann cried as the remaining longboats drew closer.

"*Gone.* Get us away from here! ROW!"

Numbly Ann obeyed, letting the current swing them around the Neck, and then pulling back in toward shore on the Atlantic side. At her feet, John coughed the water from his lungs, cursing Allender.

And Ann rowed, knowing that her brother was alive because Roger had put himself between John and Allender's bullet. She rowed only because her brother was in the boat with her. Otherwise she would have dropped the oars and let the ocean have her at last.

There was quiet exultation at the Wild Rose the next evening. John had sealed his reputation as the luckiest rogue in Marblehead, and Ann was hailed as a heroine of the Patriots' cause. Allender, foiled once more in his attempt to catch the smugglers red-handed, was further disgraced by the loss of one of his men—Roger Muir, lost at sea.

"Join us in a toast, Ann," Mr. Devane said, raising his tankard. "You've the daringest brother, the staunchest father, and the handsomest mother in town."

"And Ann's the bravest girl," John added, his eyes filled with admiration and thanks for his sister.

Ann sipped her ale but said nothing. Both she and her father wore bandages on their hands: he from his burns, she from the blisters she had of the oars. Her hands stung fiercely, but it was something to feel and she welcomed it. The rest of her was numb.

"What's amiss, Ann?" John asked her. "You're being celebrated. Can you not smile?"

She raised her head and her eyes flashed momentarily. "A man died last night."

"An Englishman," Levi Crofut said.

"And one less to kill later," added Nat.

Ann felt her stomach turn over. "Yes. At least you won't have the chance to kill him, Nat Trelawney."

Nat and John exchanged a gleeful, conspiring grin. Nat snorted into his ale, and then took a long draught of it. Ann was sickened by their celebration. Roger had saved John's life, but had no thanks for it.

And it was Roger who deserved the credit for thwarting Allender, but had no thanks for that either except a berth in the Atlantic. Ann's mind brought forth a picture of him tumbled and rolled along the sandy sea floor, his blond hair waving like the water plants, his eyes like blue shells staring up at the sky far above. She covered her face with her hand and left the room.

Her brother sauntered after her into the kitchen.

"Allender will be recalled to Boston soon, I think, to answer for this travesty," John said, cutting himself a chunk of bread. He chewed a bite and mumbled casually, "What will you say if he questions you before he goes?"

Ann sat at the table, her head in her bandaged

hands. "What will you have me say?" she asked, staring at the single tallow candle that burned on a spindle. "That Roger saved your life to prove his love of me?"

"No," John replied. He tossed the bread aside and stood behind her with his hands on her shoulders. "You won't say that, Ann."

"I won't say that," she repeated softly.

"Allender will try to bully you, though," John continued, pressing her shoulders. "He knows you were there and would twist you into a confession against me. You know nothing of what happened."

Ann closed her eyes, the burning flame still dancing before her vision. "But you know what Roger did," she whispered.

"Mayhap," John said with laugh. "Yet it didn't get him what he wanted, did it?"

Ann lunged out of her seat and whirled around to face her brother. "Can it be that you want me to hate you, John MacKenzie?"

"There's no hate between us, Ann," John said. With unusual gentleness he took her hands in his and turned them over to look at the bandages. The fire crackled in the hearth.

Then Ann slowly pulled her hands away. There was no hate in her for her brother. There was nothing at all.

Allender came in the morning, haughty and hard, daring the MacKenzies to try him further. He ordered Ann into the formal parlor and sat by the cold hearth, his tricorne on a candlestand. Ann stood before him, her face turned toward the window.

"What do you know of this matter, Ann?" the young captain began.

She looked out at the garden. A sparrow hopped among the herbs, scratching for beetles. Over her head, the floorboards creaked as someone trod the corridor, and a handful of soot trickled down the chimney. These things she noticed distantly, as though they were things remembered from a dream. Ann felt as though she had gone deaf.

Allender stood up and began to pace. "Now, Ann," he said. "I will tell you plainly. If I choose to, I can make you wretched. And I would not regret it, as you and your family have caused me nothing but trouble." He leaned both hands on the mantel and kicked at one blackened brass andiron.

Still Ann kept her gaze fixedly out the window. She paid Allender little more attention than she would pay to a fly.

"Ann, I may also use mercy toward you and toward your brother," Allender continued in a strangled voice. "If you are sensible, and begin to think better of me. The choice is yours. I'm ordered back to Boston and must make my report. Dammit, Ann!"

he shouted suddenly. "Look at me when I address you!"

Startled, Ann turned and looked at him. "You would have me love you? *You?*"

A fiery blush swept over Allender's face at her tone. "I think you did not scorn to love that Scottish peasant, Muir," he said.

"And now that he is dead I'll take *you?*" Ann laughed. "Never."

Allender swept his hat off the table and strode out of the room.

Chapter Twelve

WHEN ALLENDER HAD gone, Ann lowered herself slowly into a chair and rested her forehead on her knees. Roger was lost and dead for her sake. John was lost to her by his hardness and coldness. She herself was lost for not choosing right, for not having the faith to choose when she had the chance.

For that moment, she had doubted him. It had been a moment too long, and so she had driven him to prove himself in the only way he could. Now his bones would be brine-bleached, his body a frame for the fishes, his name washed away. She felt the enveloping silence of the inn around her, cold and lifeless as a sepulchre. The place had nothing for her now, now that Roger was dead.

"Ann?"

She heard Judith's voice. She felt the ocean

echoing in her the way it echoed in an empty shell. Her friend's footsteps came closer, and Ann felt a warm hand on her shoulder.

"Ann, won't you be consoled?"

"No," Ann whispered. She raised bleak eyes to Judith, and her tears fell silently. "There's nothing so terrible as a man lost at sea. There's nothing left on the earth to show he was ever here."

Judith's eyes filled. She knelt by Ann's side and put her arms around her. "Shh, Ann, don't think of it."

"Should I forget?" Ann sobbed. "He had no one left in the world and no home, and none here mourn him. Should I forget? Should he be altogether alone forever?"

"No," Judith said brokenly. "He did not deserve that."

Ann buried her face in her lap again, crying into her apron. There was nothing so terrible, nothing so terrible as a man lost at sea.

"If I'd agreed to go with him, he'd be alive now," Ann whispered. She scrubbed her tears hard with her apron. "And if it weren't for this damnable spite and malice between us and the king—"

"If it weren't for that, Roger would never have come here," Judith said, tenderly putting aside a stray lock of Ann's blond hair. "And you'd never have known him."

"True." Ann sighed and looked out the window

once more. The sparrows scratched in the beds of rue, the lavender raised brittle gray fingers to the sky, and the red red roses shed their petals on the ground.

"And you'll meet another."

"Never!" Ann rose abruptly from her chair and backed away. Judith looked up at her, her face pale. "I won't give my heart again. And I warn you to think twice about my brother, Judith, for he's a man who rushes into battle without heed."

Judith rose, too, her face flushed. "Don't talk that way."

"I swear it, Judith. Would you wait and see John die while you love him? Best to say farewell now, and look elsewhere." Ann hugged her arms around herself. Her legs were shaking.

Judith came to her and took her hands. "Ann, we can't choose where to love, as you know full well, for you loved Roger in spite of all. I'd rather love John for one day and lose him than to keep myself from loving him out of fear for what may happen."

Ann shook her head stubbornly.

"Ann, we can't know what may happen. We may die by our hearths as easily as we may die in battles or on the sea. You cannot guard against grief by hiding from joy," her friend said. "You only lose joy."

Ann looked down at their hands, unconvinced,

and her self-control ebbed away. Tears fell onto her bandages. "What shall I do, Judith? What shall I do?"

"I don't know," Judith said gently. "Just live. Do what you have always done."

Ann turned her face to the door and shuddered. "Out there, among all those people?"

Her friend nodded. "You cannot kill yourself with mourning, you cannot become a hermit. Only go out there, and be alive."

"Mayhap I should leave, as Bridie did," Ann said. "I know why she could not remain. I could follow her steps and start anew some other place."

"Nay, Ann, your place is with us," Judith replied, taking Ann's hand.

Ann shook her head. "You're welcome to this house, Judith, and I wish you joy of it. But I don't believe I'll see you mistress of the Wild Rose."

She walked stiffly to the door and opened it. A low murmur of men's voices reached her from the front of the house and made her pause on the threshold. But she went forward.

In the tavern, several men were taking a midday meal. They talked together, passionately, calmly, foolishly, and wisely, of politics—Crown and colony. Ann watched from under her lashes as she served beer and replenished trenchers with bread. There were many wifeless men, young men with prospects good and bad. Ann surveyed them and took their measure. She saw her mother watching her and crossed to the doorway.

"Well, Mother," she said. "Should I take your lesson?"

Mistress MacKenzie wiped her floured hands on her apron and frowned at the gathering of men. "What lesson is that?" she asked, not looking at Ann.

"Should I choose the man amongst these who cannot hurt me? A landsman who'll never stray from my side nor break my heart?"

Her mother paid her full attention now. "You have not taken my lesson aright, it seems."

"How is that?" Ann asked.

Mistress MacKenzie smiled sourly and shook her head. "It is not the man who will break your heart, Ann," she said with downcast, thoughtful eyes. " 'Tis you who will do that yourself."

Ann winced and shook her head, but her mother put a hand on her arm with unwonted gentleness. "The heart will not be bidden, Daughter. Don't you know that yet?"

Ann met her mother's eyes and felt a terrible sadness. "Then we have no choices to make," she said.

"Oh, aye, we do," her mother corrected her.

"And you regret yours."

"No." Mistress MacKenzie touched Ann's arm again and waited until Ann looked at her. "I'd kill for Matthew MacKenzie and all I owe him. I don't regret my choice, my Ann. Only see that you never regret yours."

Ann looked back at the room, her gaze traveling from man to man, over brown heads and black and blond and red, from chandler to cobbler to clerk. When the storm broke and true war began, could one of them shield her, keep her safe, preserve himself to keep her from harm?

It was impossible to choose a man she did not love, Ann knew. The very thought of such a thing made her want to weep. Her mother stood beside her, pledged and dedicated to Matthew MacKenzie, yet still unable to drive Captain Carter from her heart. Sick with sorrow, Ann opened the door to the stairs and climbed slowly up to her room.

Once there, Ann knelt by the window and put her hands on the sill. She wanted to see Roger's grass bracelet once more, to touch something he had touched, as though it alone could save her from the flood that was coming.

She gripped the board and pulled it away. The bracelet lay where she had left it, but as she lifted it out, she saw that it had already begun to fade. The green grasses had dried into straw, and as she slipped the circlet around her hand, a brittle fragment broke away from one strand.

"Ah, no, my love," Ann whispered, bowing her head. Two tears fell onto the dried grasses and melted among them. But Ann knew tears would not revive them, nor could they ever bring Roger back.

Sunlight poured in on her bowed head. The room was as still and silent as a church. With Roger's bracelet around her wrist, Ann could almost believe he was still with her. She could almost believe that when she raised her head, she would see him smile at her.

Slowly she lifted her eyes and looked out at the harbor. The *Southampton* was leaving, the sun blazing on its white sails. The following wind kicked up the foam to speed the English boat out of Marblehead. Allender was gone.

Ann smiled, knowing that Roger would have been glad that the captain had been chased away. She felt the grass bracelet shift on her arm, and with great gentleness, Ann returned the fragile token to its hiding place. She would not touch it again, but keep it safely guarded. The Wild Rose Inn had become an empty house to her now: her only home lay within the circlet.

"A pretty sight, isn't it?" came John's voice from the open door. He strolled in to look out the open window and grinned down at her. "A fine day."

"I suppose you'll take the credit for driving Allender away, now?" Ann asked, hugging her knees and leaning her head back against the secret store under the windowsill.

John contemplated his fingernails for a moment, a mischievous smile on his face. "I was never a greedy one, Ann. I don't take all the credit."

Ann looked at him and tried to remember how it had been when she waited on his every word. "What do you want, John?" she asked levelly. "I warn you, I'll not listen to you gloat and preen."

"Gloat and preen?" John raised his eyebrows as far as they would go. "Gloat and preen? I?"

Ann clenched her teeth. "What do you want?"

"I have something for you," John said, rubbing his hands together. "It fell off a British boat."

"I won't—"

John took her arm and pulled her to her feet. "Now my dancing darling, you'll be delighted with what I've got for you."

"John!" Ann freed herself from him and backed away, angry tears stinging her eyes. "Can you not leave me be? I never want to see your smuggling prizes again. I'm sick to death of all your secrets and sneaking."

"Only once more, Ann," John begged with his old sweetness. "And never let there be bitterness again between us."

Ann let her breath out slowly and shook her head. "Oh, John," she sighed.

He took her arm again, seizing the advantage. "Come. We must walk a bit. I've hidden it rarely well."

With no more resistance, Ann let her brother

lead her from the house, and along the road toward Swampscott down the coast. The air was fine and clear, and the sky open and brilliant. Each leaf and thorn on the cliffside roses was sharp and distinct, each note of birdsong rang sweetly pure. The ocean rolled away on their left, grand and great and gray to the horizon. Ann had never been so aware of the beauty around her, nor had it ever made such an ache in her. John whistled to himself, glancing at her from time to time. Ann walked beside him in silence, feeling the ground beneath her feet, smelling the salt and the sharp warm scent of dry grass as they walked over the turf. She was drifting, driven by chance, hopeless of harbor.

Then John stopped. "Do you see it?" he asked, smiling.

Ann looked around. Below them on the beach was a ramshackle hut, made of upended whale ribs and driftwood and old sails. "That's where that crazy Shippey lives," she said. "You've entrusted your goods to that fool?"

"Crazy Shippey has gone off with some Indians," John replied, taking her by the hand and leading her down among the prickly bushes, down to the sand.

The hut lay tucked into a ravine, where once a stream had raced to meet the sea. Around it was the relic of a strange hermit's life: a ring of clamshells knee-high, a poor bastion against the great ocean.

The white whale ribs formed the posts and beams of the house, and salt-stiffened canvas made the walls and roof. Ann looked at it all with a doubtful eye and waited for her brother to show her his prize so she could leave.

"Ah, I'm as foolish as Shippey himself," John suddenly cried, slapping his forehead with his hand. "I've forgotten something. Go on in, Annie. Go on and see for yourself what treasure I've got for you."

Before she could answer, he turned and scrambled back up the sandy slope and disappeared from sight. Ann stood still, the wind at her back, listening to the waves washing softly onto the beach behind her. But for the wind at her ear and the steady hush of the surf, all was silent. Ann looked at the strange hut, at the canvas door weighted down with a slab of gray wood. Her heart began suddenly to pound.

She climbed over the low wall, her dress sweeping away shells with a musical clash, and held aside the canvas door to look in.

"How—" she whispered, gripping the canvas tight.

On a pallet bed in the corner lay Roger with a splinted leg. He raised himself up on one elbow. Ann felt her knees give way.

He smiled, holding out his hand. Ann ran forward and fell into his arms.

"Oh, Ann," he said, burying his face in her hair. He held her tight.

For a long time neither of them spoke. Ann was overcome with confusion and joy. She did not know how it could be, but Roger was holding her and she could feel his heart beating against her. More than that she did not need nor care to know. The ocean outside was loud in the silence, washing, waving. Ann began to cry.

"I believed you dead," she sobbed, clutching his shirt with both hands.

"I know, I know," Roger said. He stroked her hair and wiped the tears from her cheeks and touched her lips with his fingers. "We couldn't tell you until Allender left. I'm to remain lost at sea."

Ann pressed her hands to his arms, feeling how solid and warm he was, how much alive. She shook her head. "I don't understand."

"I took John overboard, for Allender meant to shoot him," Roger explained. "And I thought I was drowned when I was swept away from the boats and was in the dark water without the sense of where land lay."

Ann shut her eyes tightly and rested her forehead against his shoulder. "Yes, go on," she whispered.

"But I was washed onto the rocks. The sea tried its best to take me back, and I broke my ankle against the rocks as I fought to stay where I was. At last I pulled myself above the tide, and there Nat found me at dawn."

"Nat!" Ann looked up in surprise. "A wonder it is he didn't cut your throat."

Roger smiled. "He meant to. But your brother stayed him."

"My brother?" Ann's heart made a great leap. "John?"

"He knew what I did, and that I loved you," Roger said. "I told him I'm for America, Ann. This is where I'll stay."

"But you can't!" Ann exclaimed, fear battling with elation in her. "Allender returns when—"

Roger put one finger to her lips. "John tells me I can go to Manchester, in the New Hampshire Colony."

"We've a cousin there," Ann agreed. "Obediah MacKenzie."

"And there I'll be a Patriot. I'm so sorry, Ann, for keeping the secret until now. But you always show plainly what is in your heart, and John would not let Allender learn I'm still living. Forgive me."

"I do," Ann said. She laughed tearfully. "But I'll throttle John."

Roger looked at Ann, his gaze so open and warm that Ann felt the heat race through her. She looked at the splints on his leg.

"And so we will no longer be enemies," she whispered.

"We never were, Ann," Roger said. "Will you

come to me there? Will you leave your home? It will be a risk, I know, for if it's known I'm a deserter—"

Ann shook her head and took his hands tightly in her own. "I cannot know what will happen," she said. "Revolution is near and war and strife and terrible griefs. Our houses may burn or be carried off by the sea. I'll say farewell to my house, and gladly. I don't choose safety anymore. I choose you."

"Come what may?" Roger whispered.

Ann looked into his eyes and nodded. "Come what may."

"You are my home, Ann," he said. "And I will be yours."

They kissed, and the ocean brought them both into safe harbor at last.

Have you met
Bridie of the Wild Rose Inn?

Sixteen-year-old Bridie MacKenzie has waited ten years in Scotland to join her parents in the Massachusetts Bay Colony. Bridie's happiness at being reunited with her family is tempered by the reality of her new life. Her loving parents work day and night to make ends meet at their small, rough inn, and they have had to give up their religion for Puritanism under the colony's law.

Spirited Bridie refuses to conform to the rules—she vows not to give up either her faith or the healing herbs she has brought from Scotland. But all that Bridie believes in, the Puritans denounce as witchcraft. The price of holding on to her convictions may be high. Must Bridie lose her new home, her reputation, and her first true love for what she believes?

ABOUT THE AUTHOR

Jennifer Armstrong is the author of many books for children and young adults, including the historical novel *Steal Away*, the Pets, Inc. series, and several picture books.

Ms. Armstrong lives in Saratoga Springs, New York, in a house more than 150 years old that is reputed to have been a tavern. In addition to writing, Ms. Armstrong raises guide-dog puppies and works in her garden, where roses grow around the garden gate.